Praise for Bad Traffick:

"Utterly gripping, compelling, edge-of-your seat writing…Highly recommended!" ~ *CNK Book Reviews*

"Written at a thrilling space, with well-drawn characters and a gripping plot, BAD TRAFFICK doesn't disappoint! It's well-worth staying up all night to reach the end. A perfect blend of emotion and suspense, Berkom takes the reader on a roller coaster of a ride. Whip fast action! Leine Basso is a woman to root for!!" ~ *Award-winning Romantic Suspense author* Mary Buckham

"An intelligent thriller worthy of the big screen… This is a fast-paced, gripping, sexy read that had me turning pages late into the night and ultimately dreading when the thrill ride would be over. I love these characters!" ~*BloodWrites*

"…Bad Traffick takes the Leine-Santiago pairing to new heights and adds a beautifully fleshed out story line full of real characters you are going to love…" ~ Ruth M. Ross, *Amazon Reviewer*

"…The writing is flawless and superb [and will] keep you reading page after page!" ~ Darlene Panzera, *bestselling author*

"…DV manages to tackle the dark side of human trafficking by taking you up to that edge but not going all the way to the dark side. Kudos to her for bringing this real problem to the forefront…" ~ Jennifer Conner, *bestselling author*

BAD TRAFFICK
A Leine Basso Thriller

DV Berkom

For Mark

ACKNOWLEDGMENTS:

Many thanks to the Polaris Project, the National Center for Missing and Exploited Children, the FBI Innocence Lost National Initiative, and several other non-profits and law enforcement agencies too numerous to mention who are working tirelessly to end child trafficking.

I would also like to thank the following people for their feedback and suggestions while writing *Bad Traffick*: Mark Lindstrom, Jenni Conner, Ali Mosa, Darlene Panzera, Wanda DeGolier, Bev Van Berkom, Larry Van Berkom, Michelle Yelland, Kim McNamara, Jen Blood, Mary Buckham, and Ruth Ross-Saucier.

CHAPTER ONE

THE GENTLEMAN IN THE IMPECCABLE ARMANI suit watched the images flash by on the screen, a glass of Macallan single malt on the gold inlay table beside him. Two additional men, shrouded in darkness and unknown to each other, were also taking part in the video conference from different areas of the world, watching the same images. Several times one or the other would raise his hand, platinum or gold watch flashing in the darkened rooms, signaling for the Seller to pause the presentation so they could look more closely at the photographs.

The Seller was visibly sweating in the air conditioned comfort of the massive hotel suite. If he didn't make the sale this time, these clients would look elsewhere for their pleasures. His reputation as the go-to guy in the business was balancing on a knife's edge. Ever since the fiasco with the televangelist two months prior, he'd kept a sharp eye on the operational side of things.

One of the executives was fidgeting, apparently bored, and the Seller's anxiety level skyrocketed. He didn't have to find a mirror to know his appearance was giving his discomfort away. He could feel the cold sweat flowing down his back and armpits, running between his buttocks. *What the hell do these guys want? Am I losing my touch?* Usually it wasn't this hard to match the client to the product.

The Seller was down to his last two photographs when all three men simultaneously motioned for him to stop. The client in Saudi Arabia rose from his chair and walked to the screen, gazing at the delicate visage.

The Seller's shoulders relaxed. He shouldn't have been worried, should've known the eyes would close the deal: jade green flecked with gold surrounding deep black pupils. Everyone who saw her stopped in their tracks. She'd reminded the Seller of a famous photo he'd seen years before in an issue of *National Geographic*. She wore the same enigmatic expression. The silence of the buyers signaled it was time for the hard sell.

"Gentleman. I see you have exquisite taste. Mara is newly acquired and in pristine condition. I guarantee she will delight you with her generous charms. As I'm sure you'll agree, she has no equal. I always save the best for last. Mustn't trot out the most sublime too quickly, eh?"

There were murmurs of agreement between the men. The Seller's anxiety morphed to excitement as he prepared to set the hook. *My God, look at them. They're practically salivating.* A bidding war would be a welcome relief.

The client in the room waved him to his side. His unusual gold pinkie ring flashed, catching the Seller's eye. He'd seen the symbol before, but was unaware of its significance.

"Her age?" he asked.

The Seller turned and glanced at the picture of the girl. Her expression still held a trace of innocence, although churning through the American foster care system for two years had taken its toll. The photographer had captured the picture before Mara realized she wasn't going home.

"Twelve years, sir."

"Pure?"

"Most assuredly."

The man nodded his approval. He glanced back at the screen and steepled his fingers, bringing them to his lips to mask his words.

"Make sure she's mine," he whispered.

The quiet statement held the promise of a lucrative payday tinged with strong warning. The Seller's mouth ran dry. He nodded as he straightened and walked to the front of the room. The cameraman panned with him, framing his head and shoulders with Mara's photograph in the background. The other two clients would see only the Seller with the girl's face behind him on screen. Taking a sip of water from a glass nearby, he cleared his throat.

"Shall we start the bidding at fifty-thousand?"

CHAPTER TWO

LEINE BASSO CHECKED HER WATCH ONE more time. *How long can a lunch take?* She'd followed him to the diner and took up position on the other side of the street, out of sight behind a minivan.

Waiting had never been her strong suit. When she was in the business working for Eric, she'd learned to pass the time until the target appeared by memorizing every detail in the immediate vicinity. In fact, many times she'd arrive days early in order to scope out the activity of the area where the hit would take place. Bus schedules, vendor movement, deliveries, residents walking their pets. Nothing escaped her notice. Her attention to every facet of the job turned out to be one of the reasons she was still alive.

But, she was no longer in the business and now her impatience was getting the better of her. Catching a glimpse of him, even if for a moment, would suffice.

What if he sees you?

She shrugged off the thought and shifted from one foot to the other. The day was warm, with one of those deceptively clear skies so prized in Los Angeles. If she didn't know better, she'd think the air was safe to breathe.

Although she hated to admit it, she was getting used to being in L.A. again. Breathtaking pollution aside, the city had a draw she'd always found hard to resist. The residents' laid-back façade masked the frenetic hive-like activity, and everyone who stayed there, rich or poor, had the attitude they were living the dream. Deceptive.

Like her life.

The door to the diner swung open and a young couple stepped onto the sidewalk. Leine checked at her momentary disappointment and took a deep breath. *Give it a rest, Leine. He'll come out eventually.*

Minutes ticked by before the door opened again. Detective Don Putnam emerged onto the sunlit sidewalk and slid on a pair of sunglasses. Santiago Jensen followed seconds later, jacket slung over his arm, dark hair tousled as if he'd only just rolled out of bed.

Leine's heart rate kicked up a notch as she watched him cross the sidewalk and open the door to the light-colored sedan. The force of her emotions rocked her, unbalancing her equilibrium. She prided herself on iron-fisted control, but when it came to Santiago Jensen the ability to think rationally deserted her without a backward glance. Viewing it as her body's ultimate betrayal, she knew enough to keep her distance. She'd be damned if she was going to add to the current problems in her life.

Or his.

Like an addict trying to kick a habit, she allowed herself the occasional glimpse. Not too close, she reminded herself. She didn't want him to know she was there. She'd done all she could to move the case against her old boss along. Once the murders were solved and Eric was behind bars, the two of them would be free to see where this attraction might take them. Until then, she had to keep her distance or Jensen could lose his detective's rank, or worse, his job.

Jensen tossed his jacket in the backseat and started to get in the car. At the last minute, he hesitated, and his head snapped up. He straightened his shoulders and slowly pivoted, scanning the block. Leine moved to the shadows as he turned toward her, but was a second too late. His eyes locked on hers.

Her heart thudded in her chest. She clenched her fists, nails digging into flesh, fighting the urge to go to him. He remained motionless, his expression like a magnet. They watched each other, neither breaking eye contact. Leine could almost hear the electricity snap between them.

The draw between them was like nothing she'd experienced with Carlos; or any other man, for that matter. It was an addiction and she was at a loss as to how to proceed. The harder she tried to forget, the more the feelings came back with an intensity she could barely endure. She woke up often having dreamt of him.

She needed to bide her time, wait until they could be together. She had to break contact or she might act on impulse and compromise the case. She wouldn't rest until Eric was behind bars. The death penalty would be too good for her scum-sucking ex-boss.

In the end, she didn't have to do anything. Putnam reached across the seat and honked the horn to get Jensen's attention. The spell disintegrated. Jensen turned to say something to Putnam.

Leine disappeared before he turned back.

CHAPTER THREE

SANTIAGO JENSEN SAT AT HIS desk in the Robbery Homicide Division offices in downtown Los Angeles and stared at his phone, fighting the urge to call Leine. Catching sight of her outside the diner brought it all back—he wanted to see her, touch her skin, smell her. He *craved* her. All the late nights working cases only kept his mind off her so long.

"Hey, Santa. Know a good security guy who can keep a secret? I got a film star needs protecting."

Startled, Jensen looked up as Walter Helmsley leaned against his desk. Helmsley was in his mid-thirties, had a curiously pallid complexion for a resident of southern California, and was on his way to capturing the geek award for most movies watched by a human being.

"What about Ben?" Jensen asked. An ex-security specialist who'd worked the Iraq war, Ben was usually available for short-term security jobs and everybody in the division knew and trusted him. With budgets stretched thin and personnel even more so, outsourcing security detail was the norm.

"He's tied up for the next couple of weeks on some rapper's detail," Walter said. "You know Ben. Likes the gangstas and their ladies."

Before Jensen could stop himself he said, "Yeah. I know somebody. She's got plenty of experience and I think she's between jobs at the moment." He had no idea if Leine would accept working a security gig, but it would give him a chance to contact her.

"She'll like this one. It's for Miles Fournier."

Jensen frowned. "Fournier. Where have I heard that name before?"

Walter snorted. "He's only the biggest thing since Johnny Depp played an effeminate guy-liner-wearing pirate." He shook his head. "Where have you been? Ever heard of Jake Dread, Intergalactic Spy? Every female I know wants to meet him, and for mostly carnal reasons. He draws a crowd that's half giggling pre-teen girls, half sex-deprived mommies."

Oh. Instantly regretting opening his mouth and suggesting Leine for the job, he realized he couldn't take it back just because he might be worried about her sleeping with some movie star. Besides, weren't most of them gay? Leine wouldn't fall for some famous pretty boy.

Would she?

"I'll give her a call. What are the particulars?" Jensen asked.

"Three guys rushed him and his friends in the lobby of the Palms."

"Not paparazzi?"

Walter shook his head. "No cameras, and the friends claim they wore guns under their jackets. Some little girl got caught in the middle when she recognized Fournier and ran into the mix. His friend committed Kung Fu or some shit on the face of one of them. Evidently, the suspects hadn't bet on anyone that was with him fighting back, and they scattered."

"What happened to the girl?"

"Disappeared."

"So Fournier came to you for security recommendations?"

Helmsley nodded. "The dude's spooked. Figures someone's out to kidnap him. Doesn't trust outside security companies, for some reason. He'll only accept a referral from LAPD. He wants one main person twenty-four-seven that he can rely on, get to know. I suggested he have someone review security around his home, maybe hire a couple of private security guards to patrol the place. He said he'd think about it. Wants our referral to do the security assessment."

"I'll see if she's interested."

CHAPTER FOUR

YURI DREADED THE IMMINENT MEETING with his boss. Beads of sweat lined his face as he huffed his way up the six flights of stairs. He viewed elevators as death traps and refused to put himself in a compromising position. Besides, no one ever took the stairs. He could come and go like a ghost.

He reached the last step, pushed open the metal fire door and stepped into the plush hallway. Expensive artwork lined the walls. A large mirror and Louis XIV side table stood at the end of the corridor. Yuri retrieved a handkerchief from his pants pocket and wiped his forehead as he made his way along the hall, careful to avoid the bruise by his right eye. He paused at the door, unsure of his reception. With a deep sigh, he pressed the buzzer.

"It's Yuri," he announced into the speaker next to the door.

The mechanism clicked and the door opened. His footsteps fell silently on the deep carpet as he walked into the suite of offices.

"Yuri. Great to see you. Come in, come in." The voice called to him from the interior of a large conference room. Yuri stuck his head inside. His boss, Greg, sat at the head of the long table, his smile fading when he saw his employee. "What the fuck happened to your face?"

"Nothing. Walked into a door. What you got there?"

Greg turned the computer tablet so Yuri could see the digital photo.

"Meet Amy—our latest acquisition."

"Very nice. She looks familiar. A little young. What is she, ten?"

"Nine, actually. Her sister works for us. You remember Selena? She was one of yours, I believe. We snapped this little hottie up as soon as we knew she was available."

Available. Interesting way to justify drugging and kidnapping the girl and forcing her to work. To Yuri, it didn't matter. He knew the way things were, and took the money his boss offered as a finder's fee. He still wasn't sure how to tell him about what happened at the hotel.

"Something wrong?" Greg asked. His light brown hair had been gelled to spike every which way—a hairstyle Yuri loathed. It made him look like some pretty boy reality show host. Still, he couldn't argue with the man's entrepreneurial abilities. Greg Kirchner had taken a fledgling career as a small time street hustler and parlayed himself into a global player on the astonishingly lucrative human trafficking market.

Yuri cleared his throat. *Fuck it.* "You know I have always been up front with you, right?"

Greg nodded, wariness crossing his features. Yuri pinched himself in the leg to give him some balls.

"We lost Mara." There. He'd said it. He watched Greg's expression, unsure how he was going to take this news. Not well, if Yuri was a betting man. The buyer was a big fish. Huge.

Greg's look morphed from shock to panic to anger in a matter of seconds. He was on his feet and across the room before Yuri knew what was happening. There was no time to protect himself as Greg's arm came down behind his head and smashed his face into the table.

"You. What?" The words exited his mouth like the crack of a rifle.

Blood trickled down Yuri's face from his broken nose, making it hard to talk. When he didn't answer, Greg let up on the pressure and Yuri slowly raised his head, leaning back to stem the flow of blood.

"We were bringing her to Mr. X's suite at the Palms when this asshole actor and his *entourage* entered the lobby." Yuri sneered when he said the word. Stupid actors in Hollywood couldn't take a shit without their *entourage*.

"And?" Greg prompted, his jaw clenched so hard Yuri swore he heard the man's teeth crack.

"She slipped free and ran toward the guy, screaming his name. We started after her, but one of the actor's guys covered him, like we were going for him, not the girl. The other guy gave me this." He pointed to his black eye. "We couldn't use the guns, would have drawn too much attention. In the confusion, she got away." Yuri's tone was earnest. "We tried, boss. I followed her, but lost her in the crowd. "

Greg took a deep breath and closed his eyes. He cracked his neck first to one side, then the other.

Opening his eyes, he stared directly at Yuri. Yuri wasn't fooled by his sudden calm. Vicious eruptions were frequent with his younger boss. He didn't dare wipe the blood from his face, afraid anything he did would incite the savagery that roiled just below the surface.

"You're going to find her, Yuri. I'm holding you responsible."

"Where do you want me to start?" Yuri knew better than to argue.

"How the fuck do I know? She's twelve, for chrissakes. She's in a strange city and doesn't have any family back in Nevada she can call. I know for a fact she doesn't trust cops, thanks to her last foster family. Put yourself in her shoes. Starting near the hotel is probably a safe bet."

"L.A. is big city. She could be anywhere."

Greg narrowed his eyes and grabbed Yuri by the throat.

"If she's not back in forty-eight hours, dickhead, consider yourself and anyone you love dead."

CHAPTER FIVE

S UNLIGHT STREAMED THROUGH THE SMALL opening in the cardboard box, waking the occupant from a restless sleep. Mara Quigg rubbed her eyes and peeked through to the alleyway. Seeing no one, she wiggled out from under the temporary shelter and stomped her feet to rid herself of the numbness from sleeping on asphalt all night. Luckily, it hadn't been very cold. Her light summer dress wasn't designed for warmth.

Trying to stay calm, she still glanced in every nook and cranny. With each step, she expected someone to jump out at her. She crept down the alley, past a garbage bin surrounded by debris, glad she hadn't seen the rats the previous night. She'd slept outside before, when her foster monster would drink too much and turn mean, but she didn't usually have to stay somewhere this dirty. Her real mother never got mean. In fact, Mara couldn't remember her ever yelling at her.

Unsure what to do next, Mara turned left out of the alleyway and walked at a slow but steady pace, alert for signs of the men who had taken her. She needed to think of a plan. She didn't know anyone in L.A. she could call for help. Hope had filled her when she saw Miles Fournier, the actor who played her favorite movie character, Jake Dread, in the hotel lobby. He'd have saved her if he knew where the man named Yuri was bringing her. She shouldn't have screamed when she ran to him. He probably thought she was a total psycho idiot now.

Thinking about Miles Fournier brought up one of the few memories she had of her mother, when she would take her to the movies. It rarely happened, since they didn't have a lot of money, but whenever Jake Dread was playing, they'd scrape up enough for two tickets. Afterward, on the way home, they'd both fantasize about how much fun it would be to live with him. Mara was certain he'd be an excellent father. His eyes were so kind. Sadness from missing her mother swept through her and she squeezed her eyes shut, trying to block the memories. She waited for the wave of emotion to pass before she opened her eyes and kept walking.

Her stomach rumbled as she passed by a small diner, the smell of fried eggs and toast reminding her she hadn't eaten since the morning before. Mara peered in the window, cupping her hand to her eyes to look inside the restaurant. A beefy man with chalk-gray hair sat at the counter with his back to her, reading the paper, an empty plate pushed to the side. The young waitress paused to top off his coffee and laughed at something he said.

Little bells hanging from the top of the door jingled as Mara entered the diner. Keeping her eyes on the floor, she walked to the counter and climbed onto a seat two down from the man. The waitress came by and slipped a plastic, double-sided menu in front of her, a rush of perfume permeating the air around her.

"Hi, sweetie. What can I get you?" she asked.

Mara stared at the menu. Tears blurred her vision as she realized she was too scared to ask for help. What if they figured out she was a runaway and called the police? Mara refused to go anywhere near a policeman. Not after what happened with her foster mother. She shook her head and pushed the menu away.

The waitress set the coffee pot on the counter and leaned toward Mara. "What's wrong, honey?" The man next to her lowered his paper and looked at her.

Mara wiped at her eyes and started to slide off the stool. "I...I forgot my money. Sorry. I'll come back later." Her foot barely reached the linoleum when the waitress touched her arm.

"It's okay. Just so happens we've got a special on breakfast today. How old are you?"

Mara turned back to the waitress and smiled shyly. "Twelve."

The waitress beamed and winked at the man. "That's the exactly right age for our special breakfast. You get a choice of eggs, any style, ham or bacon, toast, pancakes and orange juice. And, because you're twelve, it's free."

The gray-haired man smiled and nodded his head. "You're very lucky you walked in here today, young lady." His eyebrows disappeared into his shaggy hair when Mara braved a glance at him.

"You have very unusual eyes," he remarked. Mara looked at the floor, embarrassed. He turned to the waitress. "Don't you think, Rita? Jade green with gold flecks."

Rita nodded. "Gorgeous. Honey, you shouldn't hide those pretty things. I'll bet you could be a model or an actress or something, just with those peepers alone. Now, what would you like to eat?" She waited while Mara decided. Then she picked up the coffee pot and headed to the kitchen.

The man searched through his newspaper, pulled out a section and handed it to her.

"The entertainment section," he said, by way of explanation. "I always like to have something to read while I eat."

Mara accepted the paper gratefully and smoothed it out in front of her on the counter. She sucked in her breath when she saw the picture of Jake Dread on the front page and quickly read the accompanying article.

Don't miss Jake Dread live! Miles Fournier will be immortalized in cement in a special handprint ceremony this Tuesday at Grauman's Chinese Theater.

The article went on to give the time and address and other particulars. It had to be a sign. Mara asked Rita for a pen and wrote the information on the back of a napkin. When she finished her breakfast, she thanked her and the nice man, and before they could ask her any more questions, slipped out the door and disappeared.

CHAPTER SIX

LEINE LET OUT A LOW WHISTLE as she drove along the tree-lined driveway to the Spanish-style mansion. Situated in a canyon on over ten acres of prime Los Angeles real estate, the massive stucco and wood home had been built in the late nineteen-twenties by a noted architect of the time. A shady porch with arched doorways extended along the front, buttressed by square posts and sago palms. The long, sloping tile roof topped curved, pedimented gables, and reminded Leine of a Spanish hacienda in an old western she'd seen as a kid.

She parked her car on the gravel drive and got out, stretching to her full height, and filled her lungs. The rich always had the best air. The soothing sounds of an ornate, three-tiered fountain flanked by lush gardens welcomed her to the front entrance.

She walked up the sprawling brick steps to the oak and wrought iron entrance. A man dressed in black jeans, sunglasses and a dark t-shirt emerged from the shadows.

"Identification," he said.

"What, no hello, how are you?" Leine eyed the M-4 in his hands as she rummaged through her purse. "That's a tad overkill, don't you think? He's a movie star, not the president." She pulled out her wallet and flipped it open to her driver's license. "I already showed this at the front gate. Mr. Fournier is expecting me."

He glanced at the license, gave a kind of half-nod and slipped back into the shadows. At least the guy wasn't talkative.

The chimes echoed through the immense home. Leine turned to survey the grounds. The verdant landscaping held too many places for an assailant to hide, and the stone wall surrounding the property was screaming for some razor wire and motion-activated perimeter lights.

Leine could have kicked herself for taking an around-the-clock security job for some spoiled movie A-lister, but at the sound of Jensen's voice she would have agreed to jump off the Santa Monica Pier naked if he'd asked. Besides, she needed something to occupy her time other than stalking.

She was in deep, but didn't care. Jensen had become an obsession, and obsessions were new to Leine. She'd always been able to rely on cool calculation to get her out of tight spots. This was a different animal. At least the job wasn't open-ended. She only had to work it for a couple of weeks until Walter's other security guy, Ben, was available. Leine could manage that much.

She turned at the sound of the door opening. Bloodshot eyes resembling a road map of downtown L.A. scrutinized her from the dark interior, darting back and forth between her and the driveway. Leine got a whiff of fear and body odor, mixed with the sour bouquet of stale alcohol. Tequila, if she wasn't mistaken.

Shit. He's a paranoid wreck. Leine plastered a smile on her face and extended her hand.

"Mr. Fournier? Leine Basso. Walter Helmsley with the LAPD sent me?"

A hand snaked out, latched onto her elbow and drew her inside. He quickly closed the door behind her.

From what she could tell in the darkness of the foyer, Miles Fournier hadn't slept or shaved in some time. He sported a five o'clock shadow that was closer to ten-thirty and the bags under his eyes were pronounced. Dressed in a pair of gold and purple sweat pants with the name of a prominent basketball team stenciled down one leg, he completed the ensemble with an old gray t-shirt bearing the logo of a popular brand of tequila and a pair of flip flops. In one hand he held a large green Sippy cup, the other raked through his disheveled brown hair. Leine was at a loss to explain why this guy was popular. Sure, he'd be good looking if he cleaned himself up, but it took more than that to make a man interesting. *To each her own.*

"Did anyone follow you?" he asked, his anxiety palpable.

Leine swallowed the sarcastic remark that sprang to her lips and again pasted on the smile.

"No, Mr. Fournier. That's part of my job." When he gave her a blank look, she added, "To make sure I'm not followed."

"Got it." Miles paced to the sidelight next to the door and peered out, then turned abruptly and took a deep pull on his Sippy cup. Leine watched him with mild curiosity. Miles glanced at the plastic cup and held it out to her.

"Would you like some? It's a Herradura slushy."

Bingo on the tequila. "No, thanks. Who's the guy with the gun out front?"

"He's a temp I hired 'til you can get a plan in place." He took another swallow of tequila. "You do have a plan, right?"

"I will when you show me around. I'd like to get a feel for what I'm dealing with."

"Of course, yeah. This way."

He turned and staggered down the long hallway, using the wall like the bumper on a pinball machine and he was the ball. Leine sighed and shook her head as she followed.

He led her through a cavernous living room with massive beams, authentic mission-style furniture, Native American weavings, and pieces of art. The walls were made in the old way, thick with built-in niches and faced with lath and plaster. A massive river rock fireplace anchored the room to its past. All in all, a substantially built home.

They took the sweeping staircase to the second floor and he showed her each of five bedrooms and baths, all with a Spanish theme. Next, they headed to the master suite.

"You'll stay in the adjacent room," Miles said. "There's access through a door next to the closet. I'll keep it unlocked unless—"

Leine held up her hand. "There's no 'unless', Mr. Fornier. The door is to remain unlocked at all times. Seconds count." Miles appeared to consider what she'd said and shrugged.

"Fine. No locky. I'm warning you, though. When I have a lady overnight, you need to stay out, even if you hear—noises."

"As long as I've cleared her, that shouldn't be a problem."

Miles' bedroom was decorated in country French. Luxurious gold-colored floral drapes hung from tall

21

windows and over a king-sized, four-poster bed. French doors opened onto a balcony overlooking the drive. Wing-backed chairs covered in blue gingham surrounded a spindly-legged metal and glass coffee table in the center of the room. The space had a distinctly feminine feel. Leine wondered whose tastes were reflected. Neither Jensen nor Helmsley had mentioned a girlfriend.

She made a mental note to switch out the lock on the French doors with a biometrics one. Probably should replace the door altogether, she thought. The glass panes would be easy enough to break.

They finished their tour of the upstairs and headed down a level to the stainless and granite kitchen at the back of the house. Leine noted the large, single pane window above the sink and entry door with glass inserts. The only safety feature she could see was a deadbolt. A kidnapper could easily pop out the glass, reach in and unlock the door.

Miles led her outside onto a raised patio with steps leading down to lush gardens and a sparkling lap pool. A young woman wearing a hat with a floppy brim was sunbathing nude on a chaise lounge. Miles called down to her.

"Hey, Naomi. Put some fucking clothes on, will you? I have a guest." Naomi sat up, turning to see who was with Miles and smiled. She reached for the gauzy cover up next to her and put it on. Miles shook his head.

"Who's she?" Leine asked.

"A girl I met last night."

"I see."

He glanced at Leine and shifted from one foot to the other. "What?"

"I assume you had her checked out?"

"What do you mean? No, I didn't have her 'checked out'." Miles' voice rose an octave, obviously irritated. "How the hell do you check someone out when you're...you know...working it? Tell her, 'Hold on a minute, what's your social?' Or, 'Here, let me swipe your driver's license?'" He laughed. "Can you say mood killer?"

Great. He's not only a drunk—he's also an idiot. She crossed her arms in front of her chest.

"Mr. Fournier. This arrangement won't work unless you start to think like a kidnapper. What if they hired Naomi to get inside your home? Maybe unlock a door, or give them the floor plan?" Leine glanced at the now-covered Naomi, texting on her phone. "What if she's in contact with someone right now, telling them your security set up? Seriously. You need to rethink your behavior or I'm gone."

Miles' expression darkened and he looked like he was about to say something, but apparently thought better of it. He inhaled deeply and let it out before he replied, "You're right. I messed up." He glanced at Naomi, anxiety obvious on his face. "Do you think she's...?"

"Odds are she's not. I merely said it to make a point."

The look of relief was immediate. The man definitely wore his emotions on his face. Probably a requirement for an actor, Leine thought.

"Should we continue?" he asked.

Leine nodded and they descended to the lawn where she surveyed the back of the home.

There were several points of entry, depending on who was doing the entering. A pro would have no problem breaching the minimal security. Hell, a ten year-old wouldn't have a problem breaking and entering. She turned to Miles.

"Mr. Fournier. How prepared are you to secure your property? Your home is going to need extensive modifications. There will be a significant cost to do it right."

Miles took another hit off his Sippy cup and nodded.

"Yeah. Absolutely. Anything you say, Leine. Do it." He glanced at her, squinting against the sun. A small bead of sweat slid down the side of his face. "Can I call you Leine?"

"Of course," she replied. "Have there been any attempts before or since? Anyone tried to get in contact with you? Something you might consider unusual?"

Miles started walking toward the pool. "No, but I know they're after me. I can totally feel it." He shook his head. "You weren't there. They would have grabbed me if it wasn't for the fact the friend who was with me has a black belt. I'm sure they're planning to hold me for ransom. I've already made arrangements with my attorney, giving him instructions to pay whatever they want if they get to me."

"I'll do everything I can to mitigate that possibility, Mr. Fournier. Either way, you need to instruct your attorney to cooperate with law enforcement should anything happen."

"Call me Miles."

"Miles. I'll take care of securing the property. That, along with my being here on site coupled with security in front and covering the perimeter should be sufficient to take care of any need that arises."

The theme song from Miles' latest movie announced itself from inside the pocket of his sweatpants. He whipped out his phone, glanced at the screen and turned away, muttering, "I need to take this."

Leine fished a small notebook from her purse and proceeded to jot down security upgrades for the property. Motion sensor lights and cameras at strategic points around the perimeter; replace the original doors with steel core replicas and bullet-proof glass; biometric locks on all entrances and exits; motion sensitive window alarms; full complement of surveillance cameras both inside and outside the home with direct feed to her laptop.

Leine turned her attention to Miles as he shouted into the phone.

"You call that loyalty? Really? I call that bullshit. I thought we were brothers, man. Brothers don't do that kind of shit to each other. Brothers watch each other's backs." He was silent for a moment. "You know what I have to say to that? Fuck you." He viciously jabbed his finger at his phone, then stuffed it back in his sweatpants.

"Fuck."

"Something wrong?" Leine asked.

Miles' face had turned a deep shade of red during the call, but was now fading to a less alarming pink. He took several deep breaths before he replied. "No. Nothing." He nodded at the notebook Leine had in her hands. "You don't waste time."

"We'll need to get a security team in here as soon as possible. It'll make my job much easier and should help you feel safer." Maybe then he'd relax. An agitated client was much more susceptible to impractical and impulsive behavior. Her first priority was to make him feel secure. Leine was tempted to slip him a sedative, except he'd had far too much to drink. She didn't want to kill the guy.

"Mr. Fournier—" Leine began.

"Miles."

"Miles. That phone call didn't sound like 'nothing'. If I'm going to work for you, you need to trust me. Inform me of anything that occurs, phone calls, contacts, whatever, even if it doesn't seem important. Let me decide if it's nothing. Okay?"

Miles gazed at a stand of scrub oaks on the buckskin-colored hillside and took another drink. Appearing to make up his mind, he turned back to Leine.

"It was Jarvis. He's like family. Well, he was. We were out the other night and I got into it at a bar with a guy about something stupid. He took a swing at me, and I swung back. Then his friend joined in. When I looked around for Jarvis to back me up, he was nowhere in sight. He told me he'd always have my back. He didn't." Miles' cleared his throat and looked away.

"Where were your other friends?"

"It was just me and Jarvis. The thing at the hotel hadn't happened yet. Kind of cramps my style to have a bunch of people around, you know?"

"I thought you A-listers always rolled with a posse."

Miles waved his hand dismissively. "Like I said, it cramps my style. Besides, I get tired of people wanting to hang with me because I'm famous and know people."

"Well, now you have me to get between you and the hangers-on. I guarantee that won't be a problem while I'm around."

Miles smiled. It was the first genuine smile Leine had seen him use since she'd arrived.

"That's good. Did Walter explain that I need you to be my shadow? Twenty-four-seven, Leine. That's what I'm paying for."

Leine sighed. "Yes. He briefed me. I trust it doesn't extend to the bedroom?"

Miles' eyes widened for a second, then crinkled at the corners as he grinned. He wagged his finger at her and said, "I think I'm going to like you, Leine."

CHAPTER SEVEN

REALLY? YOU'RE WORKING SECURITY FOR Miles Fournier? Oh my God, mom, you've got to let me meet him." April practically squealed into the phone. Yet another reaction Leine would never have predicted from her almost twenty-one-year-old daughter.

Now that the District Attorney decided to drop manslaughter charges against April, things were progressing well between the two of them. Leine didn't think of their relationship as estranged anymore. Not after April shot and killed the psycho who had abducted her and tortured Leine.

A serial killer was as good a bonding agent as any.

The only problem now was April wanted to learn the business. To put her off, Leine told her she'd train her in self-defense to start. Couldn't hurt.

"We'll see how things go, April. The job only lasts two weeks, so I'm not promising anything. I had no idea you liked Miles Fournier."

"Are you kidding me? He's totally sexy."

"You think? I didn't get that at all."

"Oh, mom. The way you're tuned into Detective Jensen, you can't see anyone but him." April sighed. "It would do you some good to lighten up, maybe date someone else, you know."

Leine laughed. "So says my daughter who's joined at the hip with a cute geek named Cory." Cory had been instrumental in locating April after Azazel, the Serial Date Killer, abducted her. The two of them re-kindled their friendship and it developed into something more. Leine was all for it—the kid was nice and knew his way around a computer.

"Mom, can I tell you something?"

"Anything."

"I'm really glad we're back to…normal. I missed you."

Leine's heart did a joyful little flip. During her hunt for April and the killer, she'd sworn she would do everything in her power to heal their relationship, no matter what. Looked like her efforts might be working.

"Me too." Leine cleared her throat and blinked back the tears that threatened to make an appearance. "I'd better go. I have a lot of work to do before the day's over. And, yes, I'll see if there's some way for you to meet him."

"Awesome! Thanks, mom. Love you."

"Love you too, honey." The words felt strange and wonderful in her mouth. It was a good feeling to know she wasn't alone anymore. Leine had her family back.

"You ready to go?" Leine asked, watching Miles carefully comb his hair. They were about to attend their first outing together—a handprint ceremony at Grauman's Chinese Theater. Miles grumbled about all the appearances he was expected to make, but Leine could tell by the way he made sure everything was perfect, from his hair to the fit of his Brioni suit, that he was being disingenuous.

"Yeah. One more thing."

She followed him down the curved staircase to the entry hall. Miles jogged toward the kitchen while Leine checked the nine millimeter in her shoulder holster. She'd insisted Miles wear a wireless transmitter so she could remain inconspicuous at the event, fading into the background like he requested, while still keeping her eyes and ears on him. The tiny receiver she wore had a range of fifty feet. Safe was much better than sorry.

Miles returned to the foyer with a large thermos in hand. Leine eyed it warily. She sighed. *It's only two weeks, Leine.*

They walked out to the waiting limousine. Leine had ordered the car early, swept it for bugs and bombs, and ran a brief background check on the driver. She was in constant radio contact with the two guards hired to patrol the perimeter. The security company Leine hired installed most of the equipment on the estate earlier that day.

"God, I hate these things. You always have to be *on*." Miles settled back in the seat as the car began to move, opened his thermos and poured himself a healthy drink. "You want some?" he asked.

"No thanks." Leine gestured toward the mini-bar next to her. "Why not drink their stuff? Much easier than bringing your own, yes?" He couldn't be that paranoid. She'd assured him she checked everything in the car, including making sure the seals were intact on the booze.

Miles took a long draw from the glass and grinned. "It's hard to make a slushy in a limo."

They made it to the theater without incident, and the limo parked at the back entrance. Leine had checked in with the theater's administration office earlier in the day for the layout of the venue. Paparazzi, along with a throng of fans, crowded the front courtyard behind metal barriers. Notorious for his unfriendly attitude toward the photographers, even when they were invited, Miles needed to be kept far away from them.

On the way, he'd polished off the thermos filled with tequila and Leine detected a slight slur when he spoke. Hopefully he'd lay off the booze until the party afterwards. If not, he'd be über trashed by the time they left, and Leine wanted to reduce the possibility of dramatic exits. She didn't have enough of a bead on him yet to know if he'd be hard to handle. She'd read about a scuffle or two with photographers in one of the celebrity magazines, but they were prone to sensationalize. Leine needed to judge his personality for herself.

Introduced by a famous late-night comedian, Miles made his entrance onto the red-carpeted dais to enthusiastic applause, camera flashes and wolf-whistles. Leine melted into the background. Thankfully, he hid his inebriation well and appeared in control of the stage.

Contained by the metal barriers, the crowd pressed forward to get a better look at their latest movie star du jour. Several rows of chairs for VIPs stood between them and the stage. Leine had to admit, the venue evoked a nostalgic sense of movie history and reminded her of when she was a kid and her family had taken a vacation to Hollywood. The forecourt still held the same fascination for tourists as it did then.

She moved through the crowd, one ear on Miles' speech, the other tuned to what was going on around her. Leine wore dark slacks and a matching jacket, blending with on-site security, and sported a good pair of running shoes. She never wore heels on the job. Too many ways to lose your target. Leine hated when television shows and movies put women cops and investigators in stilettos when they were supposed to be working. How the hell were they supposed to stop the bad guys? Throw their shoes at them? Maim them with a sultry glance? It was hard enough to stay upright in them.

She recognized several celebrities sitting in the VIP section. As she scanned the crowd, movement to her left caught her attention. A young girl was trying to climb through a gap in the metal barrier, apparently to get to Miles.

Leine started toward her, but before she could get close enough, the girl's expression changed to one of surprise and what could only be described as panic. In an instant, she was gone, disappearing into the throng. Leine searched the crowd, looking for what or who scared her off. Two men, one with a bandage covering his nose, stuck out from the mass of pre-teens and their mothers. They both wore bulky jackets, zipped closed against the warm afternoon. Leine walked toward them, her hand instinctively moving to the gun under her jacket. She noticed a uniformed cop nearby and, thinking better of it, lowered her hand.

One of the two men glanced at her and said something to the guy with the bandage. He turned to look at her and narrowed his eyes. They immediately changed direction and started to thread back through the crowd, away from Leine.

She stopped and watched as the two men broke free from the mass of people and hurried down the sidewalk in the opposite direction of the ceremony. The little girl was nowhere to be seen. Leine wondered why the two men were after her. Her gut told her the reason wasn't good. With a job to do she turned her attention to the crowd, pushing the image of the little girl's face, along with an uneasy feeling, to the back of her mind.

Miles placed his hands into the wet cement to explosive applause, mugging for the cameras with a big grin on his face.

Mara heaved a sigh of relief as Yuri and the other man with him inexplicably turned and walked away from where she'd been hiding. That had been close. They'd almost caught her. She would have to be more careful next time. She watched the tall, pretty woman in the dark suit return to the side of the stage near Miles Fournier. Mara assumed she was a friend of his. Getting Miles' attention was a lot harder than she thought it was going to be. She had to think of a better way. If she couldn't talk to Miles, maybe she could somehow get to the woman, or someone close to him.

Now that the ceremony was over, the crowd broke up and people started to leave. The costumed characters who usually worked the area hassling tourists for money started drifting back to the forecourt, approaching anyone with a camera to pose for a fee. For a moment, Mara panicked, wondering where she was going to go. It was almost dark and she needed to find a safe place to sleep. She'd already tried going to a homeless shelter, but they wanted to know where her guardian was. Mara knew if she said she didn't have one, they'd call the police or some other agency and they'd send her back to the foster monster in Nevada. Besides that, scary people stayed there. She didn't feel safe. Miles Fournier was the only person she could trust in L.A. She had to talk to him before Yuri and the others found her again.

She sagged to the curb next to a bike rack and leaned her head on her forearms. She wished her real mother would come looking for her. The day the people came to take her away had been the worst day of Mara's life. They told her that Mara was going to live with a nice woman. Only the woman wasn't nice. Neither was her boyfriend, and he was a cop. He used to hit Mara in the stomach, telling her no one would believe her if she told because there weren't any bruises. One time, when he'd been drinking, he tried to take her clothes off. Her foster mother walked in on them and started screaming at Mara. That's when she ran away. She'd walked half way to her old apartment when the nice man offered her a ride. She knew now she shouldn't have gotten in the car, just like everyone always warned her.

"Are you okay?" One of the performers dressed as SpongeBob Square Pants stood in front of her, cartoon hands on non-existent hips.

Mara glanced up at him, tears welling in her eyes. She shook her head, unable to speak.

"Aw, man. Here—" SpongeBob held out his hand. Mara hesitated a moment, then grabbed hold and allowed him to help her to her feet.

"Are you by yourself?" SpongeBob asked as he scanned the people walking by on the sidewalk.

Mara nodded. "Y-yes." She knew she shouldn't trust anybody, but she was so tired. And besides, how could anyone who looked like SpongeBob be bad?

SpongeBob looked around once more and said, "C'mon with me, sweetheart. I'll get you set up with some hot food and a place to sleep for the night, okay?"

Mara nodded, grateful to let a grownup take control, even if he was dressed like a cartoon character.

CHAPTER EIGHT

THE AFTER-CEREMONY PARTY WAS in full swing when Miles made his entrance. Held at the Malibu beach home of an industry bigwig, the venue's understated opulence acted as the perfect backdrop to the trendy crowd of beautiful people. Leine stayed within range of the transmitter, while making herself inconspicuous. Not a difficult thing to do—as soon as people realized she wasn't famous or influential, they left her alone.

She paused for a moment at the bar and ordered club soda with lime from the bartender. A Mediterranean-looking man of medium height with an intense expression walked over and stood next to her. Leine guessed he was in his early thirties.

"They're all here, aren't they?" he said, surveying the crowd.

When Leine didn't answer, he turned to look at her. "You're new to this group." He extended his hand. "Rico Pallini. Miles Fournier's agent."

Leine shook his hand and said, "Leine Basso. Miles' security."

Pallini smiled. "Figured. You have that aura about you."

"Meaning?"

"Secure. Won't take shit off of anyone. Looks to me like you could hold your own in a fight." He took his drink from the bartender. "Am I right?"

Leine gave him half a shrug and turned her attention to where Miles chatted animatedly with a distinguished looking older man she thought she recognized.

Pallini leaned against the bar. "Miles is pretty freaked out about what happened. He said you were referred by LAPD."

"That's right." Leine replied, still watching Miles and the other man.

"Do you really think they were trying to kidnap him? I mean, Miles is an actor, if you catch my drift."

Leine turned and gave him one of her icy stares. "Mr. Pallini, I'm here because Mr. Fournier thought what happened at the hotel was a threat to his life and livelihood. I have no feelings one way or another, except that my job is to keep him safe, whatever the threat level."

Pallini raised his hands. "Whoa. I didn't mean to piss you off." His chuckle sounded more like a nervous giggle. "Seriously," he continued, "I'm glad to see he's got a professional watching his back. He looks like his old self tonight. I think that's because of you."

Or the thermos full of tequila, Leine thought. She mentally filed Pallini away as a suck up.

Miles' voice grew louder and he began to act and sound agitated. Without a word to Pallini, Leine moved toward him and the gentleman he was speaking with.

Pallini followed and grabbed her by the arm as she was about to intervene in the conversation. She turned back, anger edging out annoyance. Pallini dropped his hand and took a step back.

"That's Stone Ellison, the head of Voyeur Films. Probably the most powerful man in Hollywood right now."

"I don't care if it's Jesus H. Christ himself. My client is distressed and I need to know why." She turned back, but realized Miles had calmed down and was speaking in a more neutral tone. Leine melted back into the crowd, but remained close. Pallini stuck with her. Great, she thought. *Now I'll have to lose this idiot.*

"They're talking about an upcoming project. It's best if you steer clear."

Leine bristled, a slight twitch starting near her eye. "I'm sorry. Are you telling me how to do my job? Because I don't see anything that tells me you're qualified to give me advice. Maybe you should do whatever an agent does and leave me to do what I do. Besides," she nodded her head at Miles and Ellison, "shouldn't you be part of the conversation, protecting his interests?"

It was Pallini's turn to bristle. "Ellison wanted to talk to him alone. I'm not happy about it, but whatever Ellison wants, Ellison gets. Besides, Miles won't sign anything until I look it over." He delivered the last statement with a smug look.

"Good to know. We're clear, then? You let me do my job and I let you do yours?" Leine asked.

"Yeah. We're clear." Pallini scowled but backed off. She knew she wasn't making friends, but she had a job to do and Pallini resembled an annoying gnat with delusions of being a raptor. Granted, she hadn't quite gotten over her dislike of Hollywood types and it showed. She'd have to modify her reactions in the future if she was going to be effective in her job. Flies and honey and that kind of shit.

As the night wore on, Miles continued to drink heavily. He appeared to handle himself until well after midnight, when, in a random moment, he latched onto a young woman's breast. The woman, wearing a body hugging strapless dress and high heels, giggled drunkenly and whispered into his ear. He nodded and continued to feel her up. Another partygoer whipped out their smart phone and aimed it at the couple. Leine stepped in front of the photo taker as they were about to snap the picture and suggested to Miles they leave.

"Sure thing, Leine." He turned to the woman whose breast he still held and asked, "Seeing as how we're intimately acquainted, might I request the pleasure of your company back to my place?"

The woman giggled again and nodded, almost falling off her stilettos. Leine caught her arm to steady her. Miles let go of her breast and offered his elbow. With another giggle, she wrapped her arm in his and Leine led them through the last of the partiers to the waiting limo.

Miles and the young woman weaved their way toward the open car door and fell inside, one on top of the other. Laughter erupted from the interior. Leine stood near the door, waiting until they'd untangled themselves before she pulled out her phone.

"May I have your social security number or driver's license, please? I need to run a quick check before we leave. I'm sure you understand."

The young woman frowned slightly before lapsing back into a giggling fit. Miles laughed along with her as if she were the funniest person he'd met all evening. Leine cleared her throat.

"Your identification?" Leine repeated.

"Wait a minute...I think it's in my bag..." The woman dropped her purse on the ground outside the car, spilling the contents, and erupted in a cascade of giggles. Leine bent to retrieve the purse, wondering again at the stupidity of taking the job when Miles ordered the driver to go. The chauffeur glanced in the side mirror before slowly pulling away from Leine.

Really? Leine rolled her eyes and remained where she was, allowing the knowledge of the depth and pain of Miles' impending hangover to alleviate her annoyance at his juvenile antics. *It's only two weeks, Leine. You can do this.*

They were both in hysterics by the time they returned. The driver glanced at Leine in the rear view mirror and shrugged with an apologetic, *what was I supposed to do?* look. Leine handed the woman's purse to her, sidestepping just in time as she vomited all over herself.

"Oh, gross," Miles exclaimed, his hand covering his nose. He glanced at the night's diversion and her ruined dress, then at Leine. His look said, *do something.*

Leine sighed and called the young woman a taxi.

It was past two before they arrived back at the mansion. Leine sent the driver home, locked the front door and activated the alarm. Miles disappeared into the kitchen. He acted wired and didn't appear close to turning in yet. Leine kicked off her shoes and took off her shoulder holster, carrying it with her to the kitchen to join him.

The open refrigerator door cast a yellowish glow on the oversized kitchen island. Miles leaned against the counter, shoveling ice cream into his mouth with a spoon, a bottle of orange juice next to him. Leine walked to the other side of the counter and placed her gun on a chair nearby. Miles slid the carton of espresso mint ice cream to Leine. She opened a drawer next to her, picked out a spoon and tried a bite.

"That's good," she said, and dug into the carton for more.

Miles grabbed another container from the freezer, holding it up so she could see the label.

"Pineapple-mango-raspberry sorbet," he said, tapping his spoon against the carton. He took a bite, savoring it, and then chased it down with a swig from the orange juice. He leaned over the counter and propped himself up on his elbows, frowning at his spoon. "Y'know, when I was a little kid, ice cream was something special. I used to collect aluminum cans and turn them in for money to buy it."

"Didn't your folks believe in treats?" Leine asked, taking another spoonful from her carton.

Miles shook his head. "I was a foster kid. Got shuttled around to different families." He shrugged. "I was what they called a 'problem child'. My foster families couldn't figure out what to do with me."

"That must have been hard."

Miles took another bite of sorbet. "I can definitely say it wasn't the Brady Bunch. I did luck out one time, but I fucked up and they sent me back. Like they were returning something defective."

Leine's spoon paused mid-air. "What happened after that?"

Miles replaced the top on his sorbet and put it back in the freezer. "I ended up in a group home. Things worked out okay because they made sure everyone went to school every day, and they checked. I hated class, but loved clowning around, making people laugh. One of the teachers suggested I channel my energy into theater and recommended me to an after school drama program. They accepted me, and I took to acting like a duck to water. I could be anyone. Anyone other than the kid nobody wanted. The rest, they say, is history."

Leine slid her carton of ice cream toward Miles and he returned it to the freezer for her. "And now you have everything."

"Not really." He took another drink of the orange juice and gazed into space.

"What don't you have? People love you. You're rich and famous."

He looked at Leine. "You have family?"

"A daughter. Who wants to meet you, by the way."

Miles smiled, a little wistfully if Leine was reading him right.

"You're lucky. I don't have that. No family. No brothers, no sisters, no kids. My parents were killed in a car wreck when I was five. No one came to claim me. Essentially, I'm all I can count on. Jarvis was the closest thing I've ever had to a brother."

"That explains you being so angry the other day."

Miles reached up to undo his bow tie and unbuttoned the top buttons on his shirt. "I tried getting information on locating surviving members of my family from the foster care agency that originally placed me, but I ran into a brick wall. They either don't know or couldn't tell me."

"I'm sorry. I understand how important it is to feel like you belong somewhere." Leine felt her attitude toward him soften.

Miles cleared his throat as he reached for the orange juice. He drank some and then put it back in the refrigerator. "I think I'm going to turn in. Thanks for tonight, Leine."

"Goodnight, Miles."

Miles left for bed and Leine poured herself a glass of water from the refrigerator. His loneliness had transmitted itself and dug deep into her bones. The longing for Santiago began as a slow burn. By the time she'd checked the doors and windows along with the evening's digital feed, it had become a conflagration.

Chapter Nine

YURI HESITATED BEFORE ENTERING THE conference room. The painful result of the last time he'd met with his boss made him gun shy. Rolled gauze pads stuffed his nostrils, and the bridge of his nose was bruised and swollen, giving him the appearance of the undead. The doctor told him his face would never look the same, but for enough money he'd give him any nose he wanted. Yuri opted for the less complicated route of using ice and a handful of pain meds. Besides, he didn't doubt Greg's threat of killing him if he failed to find Mara. What did a corpse need with a perfect nose?

Greg Kirchner sat at the head of the conference table, engrossed in working on his laptop. Though Yuri dreaded telling Greg they'd lost Mara a second time, at least now he had an idea how to track her. There was one small problem. The dark-haired woman working security at the theater looked familiar and he didn't like it. He'd wracked his brain, trying to remember where he knew her from, but didn't have any luck. The memory would surface, Yuri was certain. He just had to let it simmer.

Yuri took the chair on Greg's right and remained silent.

"Did you find her?" Greg's clipped tone set Yuri's teeth on edge.

"We did."

Greg shifted in his chair and leaned toward him, interest sparking his eyes. "So where is she?"

"We lost her." A chill descended on the room. Sweat spilled down Yuri's back.

"You lost her…again?"

Yuri took a deep breath and tried to calm his racing heart. "I know how to track her, boss. Give me another couple of days. I promise I will find her."

Greg blinked rapidly. "Tell me."

"I had a hunch. I went to where Fournier was putting his handprints in cement at the Chinese theater down in Hollywood. There was a bunch of screaming kids there, and I figured Mara would maybe try to get the guy's attention like she did before at the hotel. I was right." Yuri smiled, feeling smug. "She tried to get through the fence while he was giving his speech. We never would have found her in the crowd if she hadn't done that."

"What happened?"

"Something spooked her and she ran."

"Did she see you?"

"I don't think so. We were careful. But I know she'll try again. That's two times with this actor. She's alone in a big city and the only person she thinks she can trust is him."

"That's great, Yuri. But what if she was spooked because she saw you? Do you think she's going to make the same mistake and show herself again? From now on, you're going to do things my way." Greg nodded toward the hallway. "I've got a call to make. Close the door on your way out, but stick around." He reached for his phone and hit speed dial. "We'll discuss what you're going to do as soon as I finish up here."

Yuri returned to the lobby and sat on the couch. He picked up a magazine from the coffee table. A minute later he put it back. Then he stood and began to pace.

Fifteen minutes went by before Greg called Yuri back into the conference room. He gestured toward the phone lying in the middle of the table.

"I've got someone on speaker who knows Miles Fournier very well. He has an intriguing proposal for finding the girl I want you to hear. Listen carefully. If this doesn't work, my earlier promise will come into play. I doubt you want that."

CHAPTER TEN

LEINE PRESSED THE BUTTON FOR THE third floor, arguing with herself as the elevator ascended. Miles suggested she take the night off. He promised her he wouldn't leave the house without letting her know. Rico Pallini was meeting him there that evening to go over some contracts. Otherwise, Miles intended to watch a movie and turn in early.

She'd called the security company for a temp to guard the house. Her confidence in their training gave her the green light to leave the Fournier property, but her own training and professionalism warred with her conscience.

She assured herself Miles would be fine.

The elevator doors opened and she moved quietly down the hall. It was late, well past midnight. She'd had dinner with April and Cory, and then spent the rest of the evening at the Blue Mermaid, nursing a drink, trying to talk herself out of doing what she was now doing. She paused, her hand hovering near the doorknocker, heart pounding in her chest. She marveled at her heightened awareness, reminiscent of when she was actively pursuing a target.

Similar operative parameters and sequences, she supposed.

There's no going back, Leine. If this goes as planned, it alters everything. Hesitation was never a trait she'd cultivated. Considered a weakness, uncertainty was a luxury not afforded in her previous line of work.

She wasn't about to start now.

The sharp rap of the knocker echoed through the hallway. Leine prowled the small section of hall as she waited. Unbidden, the thought there could be someone else flickered through her mind, but she shrugged off the unease. She'd deal with the matter if and when it arose.

Moments later, she sensed someone on the other side. She stepped in front of the peep hole. The locks rattled as they slid free and the door opened.

Jensen stood before her, shirtless, revealing a deeply muscled chest. A narrow trail of dark hair disappeared beneath the waistband of his partially-buttoned jeans. At first, his expression appeared relaxed from sleep. When he saw Leine, his eyes grew dark and the muscle in his jaw pulsed. They stared at each other, neither one speaking.

Vaguely aware of her shallow breathing, Leine's gaze moved from the intensity in his eyes to his strong nose and full mouth. She wet her lips with the tip of her tongue and felt the heat rise in her face as memories of the last time they were together crashed into her, erasing everything else.

She stepped forward and his warm hands encircled her waist. A groan escaped his lips as he moved to meet her. She closed her eyes and tasted his tongue, inhaled the musky scent of sleep, painting him with her body. He drew her inside the apartment and kicked the door shut, leading her through the living room to the kitchen. Leine undid the last of the buttons and slid his jeans to the floor where he stepped free of them. Jensen pushed her camisole up and over her breasts, lowering his head to suck first one, then the other. Leine leaned her head back and closed her eyes, reveling in the jolt of electricity that surged through her body.

He stepped back and she reached behind her to unzip her skirt, never taking her eyes from his. She let it drop to the floor and arched her spine, cupping her breasts with her hands, an open invitation he was only too happy to accept. Her silk bra joined the skirt and the matching thong followed. With a low growl, Jensen lifted her onto the island. The tile felt deliciously cold on her flushed skin. He bent to taste her and explored her with his fingers. Slipping her legs over his shoulders, she leaned back on her elbows with a sigh. He knew exactly where she was most sensitive, as though he'd memorized the terrain.

Inside, the tension built to an unbearable level. She gripped his hair and moaned, pulling him closer, unaware of anything but the need for release. She cried in frustration as he backed off, teasing her, toying with her self-control. Leine grabbed the back of his head and pulled him to her, feeling him smile against her.

He brought her to climax, then lifted her off the counter, spun her around and bent her over, facing away from him. Leine's skin tingled as he planted kisses along her shoulders and down her spine. She arched her back again and pushed against him.

Leine closed her eyes and bit her bottom lip as a second orgasm coursed through her. He leaned against her and groaned, shuddering as he came.

Neither moved for a moment, allowing the sensation to ebb and their breathing to return to normal. Leine relaxed into Jensen's embrace, her mind tranquil for the first time in months.

She turned in his arms and cupped his face with her hand. She wanted to remember everything about him— the laughter lines, the dark shadow of stubble along his jawline, the peaceful expression on his face as he looked at her, the complexity of emotions at play in his eyes. If he told her to leave, she'd go with no argument, satisfied the memory of their encounter would be enough for now.

Still watching her, he traced her nose and lips with his finger, then slid his hand behind her head, weaving his fingers though her hair. He brought her to him and gently kissed her mouth, parting her lips with his tongue. Leine sighed and leaned into him, returning the kiss.

She broke away first and led him to the bedroom where she slipped into the bath and turned on the shower. He followed and they took turns bathing each other, exploring, memorizing every detail. This time their lovemaking was languorous as the initial urgency had passed, leaving behind something more tangible than lust.

Finished showering, they moved to the bed and she lay in his arms, content to steal a few more moments from their separate lives, knowing them as a small reprieve.

She left him shortly before the alarm clock sounded, the silent pink of dawn beginning to reveal itself in the eastern sky.

Miles Fournier snapped awake, gasping for breath, the familiar nightmare more vivid than usual, cold sweat soaking his shirt through. Five years old again, he watched as the semi careened toward them, saw the fear frozen on his mother's face. His father reached for them both, attempting to shield them from the impact. Metal smashed against metal, the screams of a brutal demon mixed with the smell of acrid, melting-hot rubber as both drivers tried desperately to avoid the impending collision.

Disoriented, he glanced around the darkened room, focusing on the large, blank screen in front of him.

You're in the screening room, Miles, not the car. The accident took place years ago—it's over. You're safe. But he never felt safe. Shifting in his seat, his hand closed around the letter Rico gave him the night before. A dim light had broken through the clouds that hovered over him, planting in him the seed of fragile hope. He took the letter from the envelope and read it for the seventh time. *It had to be true.*

The figure next to him emitted a muffled groan and shifted position in the fully reclined theater seat.

"Hey, Rico. Wake the fuck up." Miles smacked him on the shoulder.

"Wha—where am I?" Rico Pallini shook his head to clear it from the ocean of tequila he'd consumed the night before. He stuck his tongue out of his mouth and grimaced. "Probably shouldn't have smoked that spliff on top of the slushies. Man, you gotta warn me next time you make those. They go down way too easy." Rico cleared his throat and attempted to eject himself from his chair, but fell back, slapping his hand to his head as if to keep it from splitting open and spewing his brains, or what was left of them.

"Do you think this is the real deal? You think she's actually related?"

Rico glanced at the letter and shrugged. "I don't have a clue. She included information no one else has about you. Hell, I didn't even know some of that stuff until last night."

"Exactly." Miles sprang from the seat, gripping the envelope. "I'm gonna do this. I'm gonna meet with her. Can't hurt, right?"

"What about Ms. Basso?" Rico's derisive tone conveyed his obvious dislike of the security specialist.

"I'll definitely have Leine check her out, but first I want to meet her, decide for myself whether she's who she says she is." Miles looked at Rico, amused. "You don't like Leine. Why? You pissed because she's got bigger balls?"

Rico scoffed. "Yeah, that'd happen. No, I just think she takes herself too seriously. She's arrogant."

"That's what I like about her. She doesn't take crap from anybody. She's going to teach me some moves from that Israeli Special Forces shit."

"Krav Maga?" Rico snorted. "Isn't that the fighting technique du jour? You should have her teach you Muay Thai. That rocks."

"Muay Thai is for sport, dude. I need to protect myself. Krav Maga's where I wanna be."

"Whatever." Rico rolled his eyes. He was silent for a minute, then tilted his head and looked at Miles sideways. "Think she'd teach me, too?"

Chapter Eleven

MARA WATCHED THE MAN IN the SpongeBob costume, who she now knew as Keith, open a can of soup and dump it into a small saucepan on a single-burner butane stove on the floor. The apartment was clean but sparse; a twin mattress lay on the floor by the lone window, and Mara and SpongeBob/Keith sat on two torn and rusty kitchen chairs. The small stove was the only other item in the apartment besides a sink flanked by two cupboards with the barest of eating utensils. The bathroom was down the hall. Mara didn't like how dirty the toilet was and avoided going in there as long as she could. Inch-long cockroaches skittered out of sight when she turned on the overhead light.

Keith smiled shyly, then looked back at the warming soup. "I know it ain't much, but it's off the street. You shouldn't be out there alone. There's some real bad people who like to hurt little girls." He stirred the soup with a big spoon and adjusted the stove's flame. "I'm not going to ask you why you're by yourself, but have you thought about going to the cops for help?"

"No."

"Why not?"

"I don't trust them."

Keith nodded, shifting in his seat. "Hey, I'm the last guy to trust a cop, but seems to me you need help and if I was a girl like you, I'd go talk to them. It ain't safe in L.A. Something bad could happen to you, for sure." He was silent for a moment as he stirred the soup again. "Why's a kid like you scared of cops? I mean, jeez you're what, thirteen? What kind of trouble you get into?"

"I'm twelve. Cops are mean, and they do bad things."

"Where'd you hear that?" Keith watched her for a moment. "Or did something bad happen to you?"

Mara stared at her shoes. "My foster mother's boyfriend was really bad. He told me they were all the same and I shouldn't trust them."

"Sounds to me like he was trying to keep you from snitching on him. What did he do?"

"He brought drugs for my foster mother to sell. If she didn't do it right away, he'd hit her. Sometimes he hit us kids, too. That's why I ran away. He was getting madder and madder. One time, he broke Albert's arm. Albert was one of my foster brothers," she added, by way of explanation.

"Well, I think he was exaggerating about the cop thing. I've met cops who tried to help. They've got a tough job, so sometimes they come off as mean."

"Maybe. But I don't care." Mara sat straighter in her chair. "Miles Fournier is going to help me. I just have to talk to him."

Keith whistled as he shut off the burner and removed the pan. "That's some kind of help. How you gonna do that? There's a lot of people who hang around those big movie stars and they won't let you get anywhere near 'em."

"Can you help me? You're an actor, right? Don't actors talk to other actors?"

"It don't work that way. I don't even have a SAG card."

"A what card?"

"Screen Actors Guild. You can't get work in this town without a SAG card."

"But you're working as SpongeBob Square Pants. Don't you need a card for that?"

"Not exactly." Keith chuckled. He looked thoughtful as he poured half the soup into a bowl and handed it to her, keeping his half in the saucepan. "I might be able to help you track down Miles Fournier, though. I got a friend who's got a friend who knows his publicist's dog groomer. Famous types usually have a favorite restaurant or some place they like to go. They get better service that way. Makes 'em feel important, I guess." He finished his soup and stood, reaching for the SpongeBob costume. "Time for the second shift. Take it easy, get some sleep. I'll see if I can find my friend." He looked around the empty apartment. "Sorry I don't got a TV or nothing."

"That's okay. I'm pretty tired." She smiled up at him. "Good luck. I hope you make a lot of people happy and earn lots of money."

Keith grinned. "I never thought of it that way. Lock the door behind me, okay?" He left carrying his costume over one arm.

Mara walked to the door and turned the deadbolt. She could hear him whistling down the hallway. She went to the window and sat on the sill, and looked out onto the busy street. Her heart felt like it was being squeezed so hard in her chest, it made her stomach hurt. Tears sprang to her eyes, but she stopped them before they spilled over. She didn't want to go to the bathroom alone for toilet paper to blow her nose, and there was nothing in the apartment she could use.

An older man in dirty clothes walking by on the sidewalk below looked up at her and smiled. He had a large gap where his front teeth should have been and his eyes had a wild look to them. She hurried over to the light switch and turned it off so he couldn't see her anymore.

She took a deep breath and sat on the twin mattress. Fear kept her awake well into the early morning.

CHAPTER TWELVE

"WE HIT A WALL." Don Putnam, Santiago Jensen's partner of ten years, scowled as he slapped the case folder on his desk. Jensen picked up the file and thumbed through the pages.

"Meaning?"

"Meaning the feds don't want us messing around in their backyard. They want to handle the guy their way."

"Which means the S.O.B.'s going to walk?"

Putnam slumped into a nearby chair and sighed. "I don't know. I can't believe that's how it's going to play out, but this shit's tricky. If it was one of our own, I know we'd keep it close. Can't blame 'em for doing the same."

"We're talking about a triple homicide, Putz. He can't just walk. If he does, Leine's going to have to look over her shoulder the rest of her life." Not to mention she'd continue to be considered a person of interest on three cold cases, which meant Jensen wouldn't be free to see her openly.

"Yeah, I know. It's bustin' my balls, but they assured us they'd let us know if they turn up anything about the guy." They both knew that was a wet dream. The feds treated cops like mushrooms; kept them in the dark and fed them shit.

Putnam looked at the floor and shifted uneasily in his chair.

"What?" Jensen knew his partner like he knew the neighborhood near his apartment. The Irish bulldog was keeping something from him.

"Aw, shit." Putnam glared at the ceiling, then looked Jensen in the eyes. "Might as well tell you. I don't want you finding out from some schmuck on the case. RHD's going with the Basso angle."

A spasm hit Jensen's solar plexus. "The bullet casing evidence is pretty weak, Putz. You know it and I know it."

"It's what they're focusing on. The feds never acknowledged receiving the information Leine said she sent them, so her boss is a dead-end."

"Right." Jensen shook his head in disbelief. "You know she had nothing to do with the murders, right?"

Putnam shrugged. "So you say, but you can't argue the fact that the keychain was found in her house, and that the etching on the bullet on said keychain matches the casings found at the murder scene."

Jensen had found the bullet with the unusual Asian markings in Leine's purse on a keychain, back when he and Putz were investigating the Serial Date killings. The casing matched the ones found near three unsolved murder cases Jensen had worked years before. Leine told him she kept it to remind her of her old life when she was with the Agency. She believed her boss, Eric, was the shooter, since he used ammo with a similar mark. Jensen believed her and planted the keychain where it would be found, confident she'd eventually be cleared of the crimes.

Now, that supposition seemed remote. Jensen continued to believe in her innocence; his need to do so matched by her insistence she had only eliminated people who threatened national security determined by the agency. She divulged a few details of what she'd sent to Eric's superior, but Jensen hadn't actually seen the documents. He was going to have to see her copies for himself.

Had she deceived him? Was he a victim of his own desire to believe her? He refused to allow the thought to take root in his mind. He closed the file and handed it back to Putnam.

"We're going to put the bastard away, Putz. I don't know how yet, but he's done."

The woman called Selena lay on her side on the futon in the darkened room and stared at the wall. Her chest felt as though it was about to rip apart from despair. They'd found her nine-year-old sister, Amy, and were planning to auction her off to a group of men in Saudi Arabia. Yuri, the bastard, had actually come in to thank her for telling him about her. She should've known better.

At first he'd seemed like her protector, someone who cared for her, and she'd confided her yearning to return home and see her family. But when she'd asked him to help her escape, he'd backhanded her across the face, splitting her lip, and told her how he'd mentioned her little sister to his boss. They picked her up on her way to a sleepover. Now, when the *clients* tried to kiss her and make her take them in her mouth, the pain reminded her she could trust no one.

She rose from the hard mattress and walked with difficulty to the window. Last night's 'party' had been more brutal than usual. The men had been drinking and several of them bet each other who could fuck her the hardest. When her handler had come to retrieve her at the end of the night, he'd noticed blood running down her thighs. She couldn't feel very much from the waist down.

She gazed out at the sidewalk and saw a leaf drift by with the wind. The heavy bars set into the concrete reminded her she was a prisoner. The way they treated her was like an unwanted dog. She was glad they hadn't actually put her in a kennel, like she'd seen them do with another girl.

Her life had become an endless series of horrific nights of being raped, followed by listless days spent re-reading the same magazine articles or sleeping. On occasion another girl would share her room, but it wasn't usually for long. Selena didn't know what became of them. She'd tried to make friends with a couple of them, but most were so traumatized they spent the time curled up on the bed, refusing to eat or speak.

The knock on the door sent Selena scurrying to her futon, away from the window. She knew if her captors thought she was trying to signal anyone from her room, they'd transfer her to a windowless place further inside the basement and beat her again. Not that there was much traffic to signal.

The door opened and a man with a shaved head stepped inside and closed the door. His expression was hard. She detected no warmth or human emotion in him. Her heart raced. She didn't think she would survive another night like the last one. If she died, how would she help her sister?

The man walked to her closet and started to remove the few things hanging there. Selena looked at him with alarm.

"Am I going somewhere?" *God, please don't let them kill me. I have to stay alive.*

The man pulled a plastic garbage bag from his pocket and stuffed her things inside. Then he tossed it over to her. "Get up. There's been a change of plans. We're leaving."

Selena struggled to her feet, clutching the bag of clothes in one hand. "Where are you taking me? I...I need to rest. I can't do those things again—"

"Shut up. You don't get to ask the questions around here. You're like that sack." He indicated the bag of clothes, a cruel smile on his face. "And garbage doesn't get to choose."

"Where's my sister?" She sat down on the futon. Her hands shook. "I'm not going anywhere until you tell me."

The man's face darkened as he took a step toward her. Selena felt the blood drain from her face. She twisted the bag of clothes in her hands and tears filled her eyes. He tore the clothes from her hands and grabbed her by the throat, shoving her face down on the bed.

"No. Please, don't—"

Ignoring her pleas he reached under her skirt and ripped her panties off. At the same time he unbuckled his belt and spread her legs wide. Selena screamed in pain as he entered her. The savagery with which he raped her filled her with terror. Would she finally die at the hands of this sadist? What about her sister? She was only nine years old. The thought of what her life would be like if she died before she could help her steeled her courage.

Dear God, what did I do? Why am I being punished?

There was no answer.

CHAPTER THIRTEEN

RICO PALLINI LANDED ON HIS BACK with a thud. Leine stood nearby and watched as he rolled to one side with a wheeze. She offered her hand, but Rico waved her away and with difficulty climbed to his feet.

"That's one move I'm gonna remember," Rico said as he placed his hands on his knees and tried to catch his breath. Leine had just given lesson one in self-defense to April, Rico, and Miles on the south lawn at Miles' home. Steam rose from the thick grass as the morning sun warmed the earth. Everyone had kicked off their shoes to practice barefoot.

"Then let's do it again. The only way to learn is by repetition. You want this training to be second nature so that the sequence will be automatic if you're ever attacked." Leine turned to April who was flirting with Miles again.

"April? You're next."

April reluctantly turned her attention away from the actor to her mother and stepped forward. "What do you want me to do?"

"Come up behind me and put your hand on my shoulder," Leine instructed. April did as she was told. Leine grabbed her hand, pivoted on her right foot, twisted her torso and heaved her over her shoulder, gently laying her on the ground. She did the same with Miles, explaining the movements and going over it carefully, making sure they understood. Then, it was their turn to throw Leine.

After a few tries, Miles and April got the hang of the throw, but Rico waited, insisting he wanted to watch a few more times before he performed the maneuver. When Leine was satisfied with their progress, she turned to Rico.

"Ready?"

Rico turned his back to her. "Ready."

Leine walked up behind him and placed her hand on his shoulder. Rico whirled around and thrust the base of his palm at Leine's throat, shifting his weight to his back leg while wedging his other foot behind hers in an attempt to trip her. Leine dodged the punch, then grabbed his wrist and bent his hand back until he dropped to his knees and yelled for her to stop. April hooted. Miles laughed so hard tears ran down his face. For a moment, Rico's eyes burned with what Leine could only describe as hatred. He quickly recovered and laughed along with the others.

"That'll teach you to try and turn the tables on the teacher," Miles said through guffaws.

Rico shrugged, smiling. "Hey—a guy's gotta try." He glanced at Leine.

Leine stiffened at the new coldness in his eyes. *Another freaking alpha dog. Just what I need.* There was always one in every crowd. Sighing, she continued with the self-defense lesson, showing them how to fend off attackers by using

61

their elbows, knees, and the heel of their hand on the body's most vulnerable spots, while watching Rico for more signs of aggression. Then she concentrated on teaching April techniques she could use against larger opponents.

"To free yourself from a chokehold from behind, grab onto their elbow and step to the side. At the same time bend over, twist and slide your head free," she explained, demonstrating the movement with Miles. April and Rico worked on the maneuver until they felt comfortable. When she was satisfied with their progress, Leine showed the three how to bring the same opponent to the ground and neutralize them. After that, they worked on target practice, taking turns with two guns from Miles' collection.

The housekeeper appeared carrying a tray with a pitcher of lemonade and four glasses and delivered it poolside. They sat in the shade and discussed more defense techniques. Miles insisted they have more lessons.

"I want to be able to kick anyone's ass," Miles said, leaning back in his chair, hands behind his head. "That way, if anybody tries to kidnap me, they'll have their hands full. We had a martial arts expert on set for the last movie and he taught me a lot, but I want to keep going. I'll write it off as research for Jake Dread. I might as well know how to do everything, right?"

"Yeah. Me too," Rico said.

"There are several good schools in the L.A. area. I can give you their contact information." Leine preferred to have Rico learn from someone other than her. If her suspicions were on target, he'd try to best her every time. Leine didn't have the patience. She couldn't promise she wouldn't end up putting a whole lot of hurt on the annoying asshole, which would be bad for business.

Leine took a sip of lemonade and watched the small group interact. A soft breeze ruffled April's hair as she spoke quietly with Miles. Leine wasn't sure what to make of their little flirtation. On the one hand, she didn't want to stick her nose into her daughter's life. On the other hand, she didn't want her hurt. Besides, what would happen to Cory? He was so infatuated with April, he'd be devastated if she dated someone else.

Out of the corner of her eye, a slight movement near the wall surrounding the property caught Leine's attention. She watched the area for a moment. A bird or other animal would eventually make its presence known. Once spotted, a human being would not. Leine waited a beat, then rose from her chair and turned to the group.

"I need the three of you to go inside the house. Keep it casual and don't look around, but please do it now. I'll catch up with you in a minute."

A puzzled expression appeared on Miles' face as they stood and started for the house. Leine acted as though she was tidying up the tray of lemonade, with an eye on the shadows next to the wall.

There it was again. This time a glint of metal flashed in the sunlight. She glanced at the house to make sure everyone had made it inside, then grabbed a cushion from one of the chairs and took off running toward the fence.

"Bill, meet me outside the back fence, now," she said into the mic in her ear. "We've got an intruder. Frank, you stay near the gate."

"Roger that," Bill and Frank both replied.

As she neared the block wall, she changed course and ran along its length, all the while keeping her eyes glued to the spot she'd last seen movement. Footsteps crashed through dry vegetation, transmitting the location of the assailant on the other side of the wall. Leine ran full-on toward the nearest tree, a pine with branches close enough to the ground to climb.

She secured the pillow in her teeth and scrambled up the trunk. The pillow landed on top of the razor wire she'd ordered installed on the wall. She hoisted herself up and over, dropped to the ground on the other side and pulled her gun from its holster.

Heart beating wildly in her chest, Leine crouched behind a stand of bushes and scanned the road in each direction. Nothing moved. Bill arrived a few minutes later in a jeep.

"Anything?" he asked.

She shook her head. Frank radioed that things were quiet on his end. Leine paced off the adrenaline while she and Bill searched the area.

A few yards away, she saw what looked like the imprint of the sole of a shoe. She bent down to examine the markings. The size and depth suggested a large, fairly heavy person. Looking up from the print, she scanned the ditch alongside the road, and noted a broken branch on a shrub. She walked over to see if it had snagged a fiber, but no luck. From there, the prints disappeared onto the paved road. She checked the other side, but found nothing but gravel. Bill wasn't having any luck in his search, either.

"You want a ride back?" Bill asked, after they had thoroughly scoured the area.

"Not necessary. Would you check the perimeter?"

"Sure thing." Bill said. He climbed into the jeep and drove off.

Disappointed she didn't discover more than a set of shoe prints, Leine walked back, keeping an eye on the road in case they missed something. Worst case: the intruder was casing the house, looking for the best route to abduct Miles. Other possibilities included an overzealous fan or paparazzi trying to score a lucrative photograph of Miles at home. The paparazzi angle made sense—the glint of metal she saw could have been from a camera lens. Either way, Leine would be on high alert until the week was over and the other security guard took her place.

CHAPTER FOURTEEN

YURI'S FEET ACHED FROM COVERING so many miles on concrete. How he regretted not buying the shoes with the good arch supports, having opted for the more stylish leather pair with a square toe.

He'd run a grid of the neighborhood, checking alleys and doorways, and visited most of the shelters near the theater, but had yet to score any information on Mara. It was like she didn't exist. Undaunted, Yuri kept searching. If he got to her first, then he'd be golden. Greg would give him more responsibility, which would mean more money. Soon, Yuri'd be able to bring his mother over from Ukraine. Sure, Greg's big plan to find the girl had been put into place, but Yuri's gut told him if he kept turning over rocks, eventually he'd find her. There might be a shit-load of homeless preteen girls on the streets of L.A., but none with startling eyes the color of jade.

The day was warm and the smog close to the ground. He and Ned were on their last circuit of the area. Somebody had mentioned an inversion layer on the news that morning. Yuri didn't know exactly what that meant, but whatever it was, it made it hard to breathe. Ned pulled out a dirty handkerchief and wiped his perspiring forehead. He noticed Yuri watching and offered it to him. Yuri looked away in disgust.

If it wasn't for the fact that Ned took orders with no questions and had a mean left hook, Yuri would have gone on this search alone. He found himself rolling his eyes in annoyance in Ned's choice of conversation—a lot. He did suggest checking with the homeless shelters to see if anyone had seen her, so he wasn't a complete moron.

As they rounded the corner, a sign on the sidewalk drew Yuri's attention. *Gospel Mission Homeless Center* was written across the board in block letters. A shelter they'd missed. The two men stopped and asked to see the manager.

A few minutes later, a harried-looking man in wire-rimmed glasses came down the hallway toward them and introduced himself as Heinrich Bauer, Director of Services for the homeless shelter.

"What can I do for you gentlemen?" he asked, wiping his hands on a napkin. Yuri noticed crumbs lodged in his neatly trimmed beard and realized his own stomach rumbled from lack of food.

"We're looking for my niece. Maybe you've seen her?" Yuri slipped a photo of Mara out of his pocket and gave it to Heinrich. Heinrich slid his reading glasses on and scanned the photograph. He looked at Yuri, surprise evident in his face.

"Yes, she was here a couple of nights ago, looking for a bed. When one of my staff asked her for more information, she left, quite in a hurry." He removed his glasses and slid them into his shirt pocket. "I'm sure she's the same girl. Her eyes were unforgettable. You say she's your niece?"

"Yes. We're very worried about her." Yuri shifted uncomfortably under Heinrich's steady gaze. "Do you know where she might have gone?"

He shook his head. "I'm sorry, I don't. Have you checked the other homeless shelters?"

"They haven't seen her."

"You might try speaking with the people who live and work on the street. There are those who live outside the system. L.A.'s weather isn't so cold and many find they can survive with minimal shelter. They rarely come here," Heinrich said. "I will warn you, though. They are a community unto themselves and generally stick together when an outsider breaches what they consider their turf. Obtaining information from them won't be easy."

"Where's the best place to start?" Yuri asked.

Heinrich spread his hands wide. "They're everywhere. You have but to look. Most people have trained themselves not to see them. I would suggest looking under overpasses, in the hills near the Hollywood sign, in alleyways. Some are lucky enough to acquire a costume and panhandle near the theater."

Ned scratched his head. "I thought those guys were actors."

Heinrich smiled. "So do the tourists." He waited a moment before continuing, looking at them as though he was sizing the two men up. "If you'd like, I can check to see if she's been put into the system."

"If she's been what?" Yuri asked.

"Put into the system. When a child goes missing and a report is filed, the information goes into a database which is then used by law enforcement and other agencies searching for them. Do you know when the report was filed?"

Yuri looked at Ned, hoping he'd have an answer, but he imperceptibly shook his head. Yuri turned back to Heinrich. "I think her mother did it a couple of days ago, but I'm not sure."

"Then she may already be in the database. Follow me." Heinrich turned and walked down the hallway to his office. Yuri and Ned followed.

Heinrich typed something into his computer and waited. He turned to the two men. "I'm sorry. She's not showing up, yet. Perhaps it's too soon?"

"I'll check with her mother to see when she reported her missing. Thank you." Yuri extended his hand, which Heinrich shook. The man continued to study both him and Ned. Yuri decided they'd better go.

"I hope you find her soon. The street's not a safe place for a young girl," Heinrich said.

Ned and Yuri left the shelter and walked along the boulevard, stopping at a Mexican food stand for lunch.

"Why wouldn't she be in the database?" Ned asked Yuri as he perused the menu. "It's been a while since we grabbed her."

Yuri shrugged. "She was living in a foster home. If her foster mother reported her missing, it would mean a serious cut in the money she gets."

"Really? How much do they make?"

"Depending on how many kids they have, it can be pretty good. It's all in how you use the money."

"You mean, don't spend all of it on the kid, right?"

"You got it," Yuri replied.

"Quite a racket."

"Yeah, but it doesn't pay as good as working for Greg."

While they waited for their order, a man dressed in a layer of old sweaters, a filthy button down shirt and vest pushed a shopping cart past them and stopped to check the stuff in his basket, muttering to himself. Ned nudged Yuri, indicating he should approach him. Yuri scowled, but then walked up to the man and smiled. The man clutched his cart, his expression wary.

"Don't worry, buddy. I'm not interested in your stuff. I'm interested in finding my niece." He pulled the picture of Mara out of his pocket. "She's twelve. Ever seen her?"

The homeless guy peered at the photograph and scratched his balls. His shaggy gray hair barely moved when he shook his head. "Can't say one way or t'other. Don't know. Don't care. Fuck you, and your horse." Cackling, he grabbed his cart and pushed off the curb into the street, and was almost run over by a Mercedes Benz convertible. A ball of spit and a guttural epithet flew from his mouth as he gave the offending vehicle a one-finger salute and continued pushing his cart down the street. Yuri rolled his eyes as he walked back to where Ned stood with their food.

"Fucking loony," he grumbled, taking his burrito from Ned. "Heinrich's idea stinks."

"He did say they didn't like strangers." Ned took a bite from his taco and wiped his chin with a paper napkin. "We need to try again until they get used to us asking."

An hour later, they were still trying. Yuri had mistakenly gone up to someone he thought was homeless and started a conversation, but ended up with a good-sized shiner when it turned out the man was recently released from prison and evidently didn't appreciate being lumped in with so-called street people. The contusion blended well with the now-fading bruises along the bridge of his nose and under his eyes.

Early evening shadows had begun to stretch across the forecourt of Grauman's Chinese Theater when Yuri and

Ned decided it was time to go home. Several cartoon characters stalked unsuspecting tourists, strongly suggesting a photo op in exchange for a few dollars. Yuri had made it halfway across the courtyard when Ned called for him to wait. He turned to see him speaking to somebody dressed as SpongeBob Square Pants. Ned handed SpongeBob some money and walked back to where Yuri waited for him.

Yuri laughed in disbelief. "What'd you give him money for? He didn't even take your picture."

"He says there's another guy with a SpongeBob costume who was with someone that fits Mara's description. I don't think he liked him much."

"Yeah, I'll bet. There's only room in this town for one SpongeBob, pahdnah," Yuri drawled, his Ukrainian accent more evident than its Western counterpart. "When does he come on duty?"

Ned shrugged. "These guys don't have a set shift. Depends on whether they're working another gig or made enough to score some shit. I say we wait. It's the best lead we got."

Yuri groaned. He was hot and tired and just wanted to sit down with a cold beer and watch some girl-on-girl porn. But, time was running out and if they didn't find Mara soon, hot and tired would be the least of his problems.

"Fine."

They settled down to watch the show that was Hollyweird as evening fell. Grauman's Theater and forecourt were lit up like a set from an old movie musical. The scene reminded Yuri why he'd come to Los Angeles in the first place. Like everyone else who moves to Tinsel Town with a dream of making it, Yuri had visions of becoming a huge success with cars and homes and women, able to send money back to his family in Ukraine. Reality was a cruel blow for all but the most fortunate and talented. For some, the crash came quickly. For others, including Yuri, failure made its presence known in smaller increments, wearing them down until there was no up left.

The night's festivities had gotten into full swing before the two men were rewarded for their patience. The second SpongeBob appeared around eight o'clock. SpongeBob One whistled to get their attention and pointed his big yellow hand toward the offending character. Ned and Yuri headed toward him, waiting as he finished talking with a clean-cut family of four wearing t-shirts. Each had a picture of a big potato on the front with the words *Boise, Idaho, Home of the Idaho Spuds* printed underneath.

SpongeBob Two turned toward Yuri and Ned. "Did you want a picture?"

Yuri stepped closer and showed him the photo of Mara. "I was told you might have some information about this little girl?"

The sound of Velcro ripping preceded the appearance of the young man's face as he took a look. Something in his eyes told Yuri he recognized her.

"Nope. Can't say I've seen her. A friend of yours?" SpongeBob lowered his costume so Yuri couldn't see his face.

"My niece. She's lost and we're very worried. You sure you haven't seen her? Because it kind of looked like you had."

SpongeBob Two backed away from the men but in his hurry to retreat stumbled over his costume and fell backwards onto the sidewalk. Yuri and Ned each grabbed an arm and hauled him to his feet. They started to drag him toward an alley Ned discovered earlier, SpongeBob's shoes scraping the sidewalk in a futile attempt to slow their progress. Yuri glanced behind them and caught SpongeBob One jumping up and down and waving goodbye.

"What are you doing? I swear I never saw the girl before. Let me go!" SpongeBob Two struggled, but the costume hindered any real defensive moves. Yuri worried some kid might freak out when they saw a favorite cartoon character being dragged away kicking and screaming, but he shouldn't have worried. By the time they'd hauled him out of sight of the tourists and the other characters, no one had seemed surprised by the drama. In fact, one kid even tugged on his father's arm to make him look. The father leaned down and said something into the kid's ear and moved into his line of sight, deflecting his attention to another character performing in the opposite direction.

They stopped behind a banged-up metal garbage bin, and the two men threw SpongeBob against the wall. Yuri stepped forward and landed a blow to his stomach. SpongeBob doubled over with a wheeze, his hand to his gut.

"Man, you got the wrong guy. I don't know who told you I have any information on your niece, but they were dead wrong. I never seen her in my life and believe me, I'd remember."

Yuri backed away with a sweep of his hand toward the hapless character, indicating it was Ned's turn. Ned looked at SpongeBob then back at Yuri, concern etching his meaty face.

"Aw, man. How come I have to do it? I never hit no damn cartoon character. It doesn't feel right, you know?"

Yuri glowered at Ned, grabbed the top of the foam rubber costume and yanked it over the man's head, revealing SpongeBob's diminutive operator. "What about now?"

Ned broke into a wide grin and nodded. He stepped into range and threw a couple of choice punches at the man's head and upper body. The guy raised his arms to block the hits like he'd had the shit beat out of him before. Yuri moved in behind him, grabbed his arms and yanked them back, leaving him wide open. Ned delivered a hammer blow to his solar plexus followed by an upper cut to the jaw. The man dropped to his knees, weeping.

"You cry like a woman." Yuri spat on the ground in front of him. "You remember her now?" he asked.

"Yes…no. I don't know. I can't remember."

Ned kicked him hard in the ribs. He yelped in pain and clutched at his side, slumping the rest of the way to the ground. He raised his hand to his face and wiped his nose, staring at the blood on his fingers. He glanced up at Yuri who was coming in for another go and cried out, raising his hands as a shield.

"Stop. Stop. I'll tell you." He paused, trying to catch his breath. "I met her here the night before last after Miles Fournier's handprint ceremony. She said she was alone. I let her stay at my place a couple of nights, but she left this morning. She didn't say where she was going."

Ned kicked him again. The air puffed out of him like a deflating beach ball.

"Where's your place?" Yuri demanded.

"Couple of blocks," he wheezed.

"Take us there."

Mara sat by the window in the small apartment, wondering how she was going to get to the restaurant Keith's friend said was Miles Fournier's favorite place to eat. The place wasn't on a major bus line. Even so, she didn't have money for the fare. She glanced at the street and noticed Keith halfway down the block walking toward the apartment building with two men who looked familiar. She leaned closer to the window, trying to make out who he was with. Keith was bent over and limping. Alarm bells went off in her head when she realized the taller person to his right had the same gait and posture as the man she knew as Yuri.

Mara stood, then sat back down in the chair, unsure what to do. Panic rose in her throat and she couldn't take a deep breath. Her heart fluttered in her chest, and she stood again. She ran to the door, unlocked the locks and bolted down the hallway to the dreaded bathroom. She tried the handle, but it was locked. Terror gripped her and she pounded her small fist against the door, yelling at whoever was inside to please hurry.

Finally, the toilet flushed and the handle turned. The door opened and an overweight, gray-haired man with large, horn-rimmed glasses and a newspaper in his hand walked out, a stern look on his face.

"Where the hell are your manners? Don't you know it's rude to interrupt someone taking a shit?"

Ignoring him, Mara ran inside the bathroom and slammed the door shut. The assault on her nostrils was immediate. Her eyes teared and she held her breath, to no avail. She opened the cabinet over the sink, looking for room deodorant, but all she found was a scummy bar of hotel soap. She held it to her nose and breathed in a cautious breath. Men's voices floated up the stairwell and

Mara's heart skipped. She stepped inside the grungy shower and closed the curtain.

Mara listened as their footsteps passed the bathroom and continued down the hallway. Keith was speaking loudly enough that Mara would have been able to hear him even if she was still in the apartment. He was trying to warn her.

The sound of the key in the lock followed by the apartment door opening and closing told Mara it was time to move. As quietly as she could, she cracked open the bathroom door and peeked into the hall, making sure Keith and the two men or the angry man from earlier weren't visible. Satisfied no one would see her, Mara slipped out of the bathroom and fled down the stairs and out the front doors, careful to turn right and go around the building where they wouldn't be able to see her from the window in the apartment. She was worried for Keith, but knew she couldn't risk looking for him later to thank him or say goodbye.

She stopped for a moment to catch her breath, and realized she was in the same predicament as before, with nowhere to go. That's not true, she corrected herself. She knew where Miles Fournier's favorite restaurant was.

She just had to think of a way to get there.

CHAPTER FIFTEEN

"HEY, LEINE. CAN YOU COME in here?" Miles called from the living room.

"Be there in a minute," Leine replied. She'd just gotten off the phone with Walter Helmsley of the LAPD. The relief security guy, Ben, wouldn't be available for another couple of weeks and he'd asked her to stay on as Miles' bodyguard until then. Not enthusiastic about babysitting Miles, she'd asked him if there was someone else they could use, but Walter told her they were short-handed. Against her better judgment, she agreed to stay on. With a deep sigh, she took a drink from her water bottle and made her way to the cavernous living room.

The space was one of her favorites in the mansion. The huge rock fireplace held the soot from decades of fires, dating back to when it was used as the main source of heat. To Leine it defined the constancy of home life, of which she had none at the moment. The furniture was comfortable, some with intricate Navajo weavings draped over the back, and married well with the Spanish fabric on the cushions. Leine would sometimes go in there after Miles went to bed to revel in the solitude.

She rounded the corner and walked down the steps to the main part of the room. Miles sat on the massive sofa speaking to a dark-haired woman with her back to Leine.

How the hell did she get past the security guard at the gate? The guards had explicit instructions to contact Leine regarding all arrivals. Wary, she skirted the sofa and stood in front of Miles and his guest.

"Leine Basso, I'd like you to meet Jean Quigg, my half-sister."

Leine extended her hand as her mind raced for context. Jean shook it with a tentative smile, her palm clammy. Deep lines etched the space between her eyebrows and highlighted the dark circles under her eyes, the color of which matched an ugly bruise on her left cheekbone. She made fluttery movements with her hands, as though she wasn't sure what to do with them. She reminded Leine of domestic violence victims she'd met.

Jean was pretty in a conventional way, with blue-green eyes, her medium brown hair swept back in a comb. She wore a knock-off designer sundress. Leine estimated her to be somewhere in her mid- to late-twenties, although she could have been younger; it was possible she'd aged from stress. Being physically abused could do that to a person.

"Nice to meet you," Jean said. "Miles tells me you're his body guard?"

"That's correct." Leine had a seat in the armchair across from them. "Excuse my confusion, but I was under the impression Miles was an only child and his parents were killed in a car accident years ago. How is it you're related?"

They exchanged glances and Jean nudged Miles with her hand. "You tell her. I'm still blown away."

Miles sat forward on the couch, excitement lighting his face. "This is so cool, Leine. Jean is my father's daughter from an earlier relationship. She says her mother didn't tell her until a few months ago who her father was since he left them before she was born. Apparently, he sent money every month until he died."

Jean picked up the conversation. "When the payments stopped, my mother assumed the worst. It wasn't until later that she told me his name. I did some research on the Internet and found out Miles' parents were killed in a horrible car accident about the same time the money to my mother stopped. Since my father and Miles have the same last name, I wondered if there was a connection." Jean glanced at Miles who nodded for her to continue. "A few months ago, my mother found out she had inoperable breast cancer. Time was running out. I asked her if she knew if Miles and my father were related. She said he was my half-brother and that she'd written to the foster care agency he was placed with to make sure he had everything he needed. She kept track of him through the years. She felt sorry for him losing his parents so young."

"I see." Leine watched Jean closely. Her nervousness, though somewhat suspicious, could be explained as an effect from meeting her famous half-brother for the first time, or, it could be left-over mannerisms from the possible domestic violence. As yet unconvinced, Leine continued. "So if Miles were to contact the agency, they'd confirm your mother's support?"

Without skipping a beat, Jean replied. "Yes, I think so, unless she requested the information to be private." She hesitated a moment before continuing. "I know this sounds far-fetched and Miles probably gets a million people trying to contact him who claim to be related, but I know in my heart he's my brother." Jean turned shining eyes toward Miles.

Miles patted Jean's hand and glanced at Leine. "Jean's going to be staying with us for a while."

Leine kept her expression impassive. "Can I speak to you for a minute?"

"Yeah, sure. Would you excuse us, Jean?"

Jean smiled tentatively as Miles got up from the sofa and followed Leine out of the room. "What's up?"

Leine pivoted and took a step closer so she was within inches of Miles' face. "Did you forget why you hired me?" she asked, her voice low.

"Of course not. What's wrong?" He took a step back, wariness moving across his face like a wave.

"Some woman shows up out of the blue, claims to be your sister and you immediately invite her to live with you? Have you lost your mind? Last time I checked, you were convinced someone was out to kidnap you. Don't you think Jean's timing is a tad suspicious?" Leine shook her head in exasperation as she crossed her arms and started to pace. "How the hell did she get through to you? It can't be easy."

"The letter came through Rico. He gets mail from my fans and determines which ones I should respond to. He thought this was something I would want to see."

"You should have come to me as soon as you got the letter." Leine stopped pacing and stood in front of Miles. "I can't work like this, Miles. You have to meet me part way here."

"It's not like that." Miles' eyes pleaded with her to believe him. "She told me stuff only I know."

"Like?" Leine resumed pacing.

"Like the names of all of my foster parents. And she knew the name of my favorite stuffed animal when I was eight years old."

"You sure that info never made it into some interview you gave? Or, how about one of your friends, or foster parents? You can't possibly remember everything you ever said or know what someone else may have told an interviewer."

The concentration line between Miles' eyes deepened into a frown. "Look. I'll be honest with you. There's more. She's trying to find her daughter. Some thugs kidnapped her and Jean's afraid of what they'll do. Did you see the bruise on her face? They smacked her around when she ran after them, told her they'd kill her if she tried anything."

Leine stopped mid-stride. "They took her daughter?"

"Yeah. She knew she had to contact me because I have the resources and contacts to help her. She thought because we were related I'd be more inclined to help her."

"How did they take her?"

"Child protective services took the kid away from her and put her into foster care. Even though she wasn't supposed to go near her, Jean made a habit of following her to school and back, to make sure she was all right. The kid ran away from the foster home one night and Jean followed her. She saw a van pull over and she got in. Jean followed, thinking it might be someone her daughter knew, but when they got to the highway and kept going, she realized Mara was in trouble. She followed the van to a gas station just outside of LA and confronted them, but one of them beat her pretty bad. They took off."

"Did she go to the police?"

"She can't. They told her if she did, she'd never see her daughter again, that they have a contact in the LAPD and would know."

"They don't want money?"

"No. They want the girl."

"Traffickers."

Miles sighed. "She thinks so. God, Leine. You know what those bastards do with twelve-year-old girls?"

Leine nodded. "LAPD has a unit dedicated to human trafficking. She should start there. I'm sure they've worked this kind of case before and will know how to proceed."

"No. Jean was adamant. No police."

"They could have told her they had a source in the department to scare her." Leine sighed. *Shit.* She was going to have to take Miles' word for it—for the moment. "Let me make some inquiries, see if I can find out about the people who took her. I'm going to need to talk with her, see if she knows more than she thinks."

"You're awesome, Leine." Miles wrapped his arms around her in a hug, then let go with a cough, his face red. Leine raised an eyebrow.

"You do know I'll need to run a security check on her. And, I'm going to get her DNA tested to determine if she really is related."

Miles smiled, obviously relieved to move on from the hug. "Check away, Leine. She's my sister, I'm sure of it."

Leine managed to pry tiny bits of information out of Jean, but it wasn't much to go on. The woman was obviously terrified of crossing the men who took her daughter. So much for the domestic violence angle. These guys sounded like they knew what they were doing and didn't have a problem using any means to get what they wanted.

"I never would have lost Mara if it wasn't for the booze," Jean said.

"What happened?" Leine asked.

She took a deep breath and let it out, slowly. "I'm a binge drinker. I have a tendency to blackout for days at a time." She looked down at her hands. "I left Mara...alone a couple of times. The neighbor noticed and called Child Protective Services. They took her away."

"Miles told me how they picked her up off the street. Did you get the license plate number on the van?"

Jean nodded. "I did. But now I can't find the piece of paper I wrote it on." She closed her eyes. "I thought I put it in my purse, but it's not there." A tear slid down her cheek.

Leine felt some of the hardness she'd been harboring toward Jean soften. She figured she'd had enough questioning for the day and rose to leave. Jean grabbed her hand.

"Please help me find her, Leine. She's the only thing I've got. We—" Jean's voice cracked. "She was so angry with me for not being able to stop them from putting her in foster care." She raised imploring eyes to Leine. "I'd do anything to get her back. I have to regain her trust."

Leine shifted uncomfortably as the memories from her own life flooded back. She'd had a similar relationship with her daughter, April, before the Serial Date killer abducted her and used her to lure Leine into his web of sick games and grisly murders. In the aftermath, she and April's relationship had slowly begun to heal as they rebuilt the solid mother-daughter bond they'd enjoyed years before.

"Here. Take this. It's the one picture I have with me." Jean reached into the pocket of her dress and pulled out a much-handled photograph of her daughter. She handed it to Leine. Leine glanced at the enigmatic expression on the photograph and her breath caught: it was the same girl from Miles' handprint ceremony.

"I've seen her. She was trying to get through the barriers at one of Miles' events."

Jean frowned, looking at Leine. "How could that be?"

"I'm sure it's her. There were two men in the crowd who appeared to be looking for her. By the look on her face she saw them, got scared, and disappeared."

Jean stood, hugging her arms. "You mean she escaped?" She started to pace, her head down, lost in thought. "We've got to find her. She won't be able to survive out there by herself. She was trying to get to Miles, I know it. He's her favorite actor. She doesn't know anyone in L.A., so of course she would try to get his attention." She stopped and stared at Leine, large eyes dark against a white face. "We're the only chance she's got. You've got to help me."

"I'll do what I can, Jean."

Chapter Sixteen

I T WAS PAST NOON BY THE time Leine reached DNAsty Labs with the saliva sample from Miles and hair from Jean's brush. Though it had taken some doing, she'd convinced Miles it was better to do the initial screen without Jean's knowledge in case she wasn't who she said she was, got nervous and did something stupid.

A standard background check didn't reveal anything other than what Jean had told her, but Leine still wasn't convinced. Call it a gut reaction, call it cynicism, but she rarely took anyone at face value. Especially someone who conveniently discovered she was Miles Fournier's half-sister the same time someone allegedly tried to kidnap him.

The attractive, sandy-haired woman behind the counter was different than the person Leine remembered from before when she'd brought in a severed finger to be tested to make sure it wasn't her daughter's. Leine smiled as she approached the desk.

"My name is Leine Basso. Is Zephyr Cain available? I'm an old friend." Zephyr and Leine went way back to when she and Carlos, an assassin she'd been involved with, both worked for the Agency. Zephyr had been a lab tech at the time—now he was acting CEO of DNAsty Laboratories.

"Just a minute, I'll check," the woman said. She pressed a button on her phone and spoke into a headset. "A Leine Basso's here to see you? All right, I'll send her back." She smiled at Leine. "He's through those doors, down the hall, third door on the left."

"Thanks." Leine walked through the double glass doors and along the hallway, following the pulsing percussion of Paper Thin by John Hiatt. The music had to be coming from Zephyr's office.

She was right. Zephyr sat at his desk playing an imaginary set of drums with a pencil in each hand, head of curly dark hair bobbing, lost in the beat from an impressive set of speakers on the surfboard-flanked bookshelf behind him. He grinned when he saw Leine, jumped out of his chair and threw his arms around her in a breath-defying bear hug. Leine hugged him back and laughed.

"Good to see you, Leine," he said. His eyes twinkled behind a pair of black nerd glasses. "To what do I owe this most auspicious visit?" The smile faded and he grew serious. "Not another finger?"

"No, not another finger, Zeph. I need to know if these two people are related." Leine opened her purse and took out two plastic containers. "This one's a cheek swab. The other one's hair."

"Easy enough. When do you need it? Is this a matter of life or death like the last one, or can I have a little time? We're really backed up." Zephyr crossed the room and reached over to turn down the volume on his iPod.

"I'd like to have the results as soon as possible, but it isn't life or death." At least, not at the moment.

"Will a few days' work?"

"Perfect."

"So how are you? I mean, I heard about April and that sadistic fuck who kidnapped her. How's she doing?" He returned to his desk, giving her a meaningful look. "It's not every day you kill a psychopath. The whole thing must have been mind-altering."

Leine rubbed the back of her neck. "Mind-altering in a good way. April and I are back on track. Azazel's dead and the case is closed."

Zephyr drummed his fingers on the desk with a look that said he wasn't sure whether to say what was on his mind.

"What? I know that look, Zeph."

The drumming stopped and Zephyr cleared his throat. "I don't know if this is important, but I heard some stuff on the old Agency grapevine. Stuff about you."

"And?"

"That the feds are building a case against you for three murders that happened in L.A. years ago."

"Let's just say I'm a person of interest. And no, I didn't kill the men in question."

Zephyr's frown told her there was more to the story. She waited in silence.

"Yeah, that's not what I heard. I heard you're the main suspect and that Eric's boss pulled out the stops in the investigation. He went ballistic when he found out you told the LAPD Eric was the shooter. Dude—" Zephyr shook his head, his expression serious. "You gotta watch yourself with these guys. You're staring into the massive jaw of a great white on this one."

"Good to know. I wasn't aware of that." Why hadn't Jensen told her? Christ, if he didn't want to risk a phone call he could have gotten his partner, Putnam to do it. Eric must have intercepted the information Leine sent to his boss. The files listed the multitudes of sins he'd committed off the books while he pocketed exorbitant fees and used Agency resources. The information conjured up a whole host of problems, not the least of which included the real possibility of a multiple-murder conviction. California wasn't afraid of the death penalty. Leine looked at Zephyr. Her chest tightened at the concern on his face.

"Thought you should know," Zephyr said. "And be careful of Eric, man. He's a few clowns short of a circus, if you know what I mean. He'd just as soon kill you as know you're out there gunning for him."

He had a point. Trained as an assassin, being hyper-alert and aware of her surroundings had become second nature, with danger a close ally. She'd always run under the radar, not subject to the United States legal system or any other country, for that matter.

But now she was on her own. There'd be no Agency to watch her back, no Carlos to commiserate with. Even Jensen wasn't available. In the eyes of the Agency, isolated and uncontrolled tended to be a potent and dangerous combination. If the Agency continued along the avenue they were headed now and the LAPD brought charges against her, chances were good Leine would have to go to ground, yesterday. The Agency was not a sympathetic entity. She'd be as good as dead.

If that happened, Leine would be running for the rest of her life.

CHAPTER SEVENTEEN

THE HOUSE ON MULHOLLAND was perfect.

The video equipment, lighting and audio had already been delivered and put in place for Ellison's pet project. Twenty-four-hour security had been hired to monitor the front gate remotely to keep crashers from showing up unannounced. All he needed now was his star attraction. That, and his small, hand-picked film crew.

The town car sped past the elegant, towering eucalyptus trees that lined the driveway as his driver maneuvered back down the mountain toward Malibu. Ellison barely noticed the awe-inspiring view of the ocean in the distance.

He was not a man who waited, and he'd had to wait. The fact that his latest acquisition was temporarily unavailable set his blood to a rolling boil. He'd paid a premium and expected immediate delivery. Ellison punched the new number into his phone and leaned his head against the leather headrest with an irritated sigh. Two rings...three rings...four rings. The shit heel still didn't pick up. Ellison ended the call and slammed down the phone. The person he was trying to reach wasn't under contract—all business was done on a handshake. The implied threat of severe repercussions should things go south was the only deterrent to the deal falling through.

Things couldn't have gone further south if he'd flown to Antarctica.

Impatient, Ellison reached over to the console and pressed the button to open the DVD tray. He selected one of his favorites, popped it into the holder and pressed play. The scene opened on a well-lit bedroom with two doors. Sensuous music played in the background. The door on the left opened and a man in his late fifties walked in, holding the hand of a young girl wearing a frilly sundress. At that moment, Ellison's phone rang. Annoyed at the interruption, he glanced at caller I.D. It was the number he'd just called.

Ellison stopped the video and answered the phone. "Where the hell have you been?"

"I was on the other line with our friend," the voice replied. "He says he's close and needs more time. I told him that was fine, but that the other option had been put into place. Everything's working as planned, Stone. I promise to have you back up and running within the week."

"I'd better be. You know the consequences if it doesn't happen." Ellison disconnected and gazed out the window, absentmindedly twisting the gold ring on his pinkie finger. He could envision her eyes; those beautiful, haunting eyes. He sensed victory. Sweet, heavenly victory.

Soon, my angel. Soon.

Leine placed her purse on the chair next to her and sat down. A poster of a young girl with wide, innocent eyes and the words "For Sale" printed in bold red across the bottom stared at her from a wall of the small office. On the other side, hundreds of push pins pierced holes through a large map of the world, with several countries a riot of color. She watched her old friend Lou Stokes across the desk as he worked his magic on the computer in front of him.

Previously a weapons and explosives expert at the Agency, Lou was currently head of SHEN—Stop Human Enslavement Now, an international non-profit organization working to end modern-day slavery. In his mid-sixties with a slight paunch that affirmed his love of fine wine and rich food, Lou had a no-nonsense vibe and practical approach that Leine trusted. What you saw was what you got with Lou.

He peered through his bifocals and tapped the screen in front of him. "Here's what I wanted to show you. Take a gander at the statistics." He turned the monitor so Leine could see what he was talking about.

"It says between two and four million children a year as young as four are commonly kidnapped and sold into the sex trade." Leine glanced at Lou for verification.

He nodded. "It's worse than that. That's the best estimate. The use of children as sex slaves has grown exponentially, especially with the spread of HIV, hepatitis and other communicable diseases. In some countries, it's thought a virgin will actually cure an HIV infection." Lou leaned back in his chair and rubbed his eyes, the toll of the job evident in his weary expression. "When you bring one ring of traffickers down, three pop up in its place. It ain't a job for the faint hearted."

"Which is more prevalent—labor or sex slavery?" Leine asked.

Lou sighed. "Depends. It runs the gamut—anywhere from domestic servants for the rich to agricultural workers, to running prostitutes; all held against their will without access to identification or money. Victims often can't speak the language of the country where they've been trafficked and many of them suffer horrific violence at the hands of the traffickers." He stared at the computer screen as though it held answers. "And we thought slavery was abolished with the Civil War. I'll tell you, Leine, it's more insidious than ever. Sex trafficking alone brings in tens of billions annually in developed countries. With money like that, I don't see it going away anytime soon."

"What kinds of resources are in place for the victims?"

Lou leaned forward, placing his elbows on the desk. "There's a national hotline, staffed twenty-four-seven. Larger law enforcement agencies have taken the lead and created specialized task forces to deal with this issue, especially those with ports. Laws have been passed in all but a handful of states, and we're working on those. Then there's us, the Polaris Project, Human Trafficking Network, Truckers Against Trafficking and several other non-profits. There's been a huge push to integrate data and resources within the FBI, ICE and local police and sheriff departments." Lou cocked his head to the side. "You got a dog in this race?"

"In a way. I met a woman who's convinced her daughter was kidnapped by traffickers. I've spoken with her at length to try to get a sense of what she knows and what she doesn't."

"How old's the daughter?"

"Twelve."

"The average age of children sold into prostitution is twelve. Have you contacted LAPD? They've got a good Human Trafficking Unit."

Leine shook her head. "The woman is terrified of going to the authorities with this. Says the kidnappers told her they've got connections and will know if she talks to anyone, that they'll sell the kid to the highest bidder and she'll never see her again."

"She never will see her again if something isn't done. At least give me a description of the girl. I'll keep an eye out in case something comes across my desk."

Leine removed a copy of the picture Jean gave her and handed it to Lou. "I'm pretty sure I saw her a couple of days ago in West Hollywood, near Grauman's."

"They already turned her out?"

Leine shook her head. "I think she escaped. There were a couple of men who looked like they might be after her, but they took off when they realized I'd seen them."

Lou nodded. "One of them was probably her pimp. Could be she escaped, but if they were that close it won't last. What's her name?" he asked, looking at the print.

"Mara. The mother thinks the kidnappers are Russian."

"Why is that?"

"She said one of them had an accent like Putin."

Lou sighed. "That narrows things down, but not by much. The Russian mafia's heavy into the trade, but their victims are usually from Eastern Europe, not American kids. It's not unheard of, though. I'll check around, work some of my contacts, see if I can find any leads." He paused and squeezed his eyes shut. Then he snapped forward, eyes open and started to type, his fingers flying across the keyboard.

"What?" Leine asked.

"One of the homeless shelters downtown put in a report a little while ago about an unaccompanied minor who I think matches the picture. The guy who filed the report mentioned unusual eyes." He leaned toward the monitor while he waited for the data to populate the screen. A couple of seconds later, he snapped his fingers.

"Looks like your Mara escaped and is on her own in downtown L.A. At least, she was the day this report was filed." He read a little further. Lou glanced at Leine, his expression grave. "It also mentions two men stopped at the shelter with her picture. They claimed she was a niece and were quite concerned that they find her."

"The traffickers. Is there a description?" Leine asked.

Lou nodded. "Says here the one who claimed to be her uncle had an Eastern European accent and a bandage on his face."

"Bingo." Leine's heart rate kicked up a notch as things fell into place. One of the men she'd noticed that day wore a bandage across his nose.

"We have to find her before they do." Leine grabbed her car keys off the desk and stood to leave.

"I'll put out the word. We've got people working the street, looking for runaways. The more eyes the better." Lou slid a handful of business cards across the desk toward her. "Here's my personal cell. The twenty-four hour hotline is listed, too. Call me if you need anything."

"I will. Thanks, Lou."

Leine returned to her car, deep in thought, imagining how afraid Mara must be, alone and lost in a huge city like L.A. Not only did she have that seemingly insurmountable barrier, but there were some pretty evil people looking for her. She thought of April, and pulled out her phone. April answered on the first ring.

"Hey, mom. What's up?"

"Hey." Leine cleared her throat. "Just wanted to check in with you, see how things are going." Ever since she and April had reunited after years of estrangement, each conversation with her daughter had the emotional effect of a cannon ball hitting her in the solar plexus. In a good way.

"Things are great. Just like they were last night when you called me," April teased. She waited a beat before continuing. "What's wrong? You don't usually call with nothing to talk about."

"It's nothing. I...I just wanted to hear your voice."

April's gentle chuckle floated through the phone. "Baloney. What's the real reason? Did you see an adorable puppy and think of me or something?"

Leine laughed. "No. It's just that you're so important to me and I wanted you to know. I recently found out about a twelve-year-old girl who is alone in L.A. and very, very scared. The girl's mother is looking for her and it made me think of what I would have done if the situation were reversed and I was looking for you." She cleared her throat again, emotion rising to the surface. "That's all."

"That's all? That's a lot, mom. Especially after what we went through. So who's the girl and how did you find out about her?"

"A woman claiming to be Miles Fournier's sister is looking for her. At first we thought traffickers had her, but it appears she escaped and is on her own."

April inhaled audibly. "In L.A.? That's gotta be stupid scary for her. What can we do?"

"I'm working on it. I just had a conversation with an old friend of mine and he's putting the word out on her."

"Can't you do anything more?" April asked.

"Like I said, I'm working on it."

"I have faith in you, mom. If anyone can find her, it's you."

Leine hoped she was right.

CHAPTER EIGHTEEN

"HEY HONEY, YOU LOST?"

"No." Mara shook her head as she studied the sidewalk and tried to avoid direct eye contact with the woman in the short skirt and five-inch stilettos.

The lady followed behind her, a lit cigarette between her bright, fuchsia-colored lips. "You sure, baby? You look lost."

"No, I'm fine. I need to go home. I...I just took the wrong bus."

"I'll say. You ain't in Kansas anymore." The prostitute laughed at her own joke. "Listen," she continued. "Big brother Bobby over there will take care of you. Protect your skinny white ass, cause it's gonna need protectin' you stay around here long, you feel me?"

Mara stepped up the pace and told herself to stay calm. She turned to see how close the lady was and stifled a scream when she caught sight of Bobby not far behind her with a determined look on his face.

Mara broke into a run. Bobby swore and started after her, his shoes slapping the pavement as he ran. Terror welled up in Mara's throat, making it hard to scream.

"Come here, now. I ain't gonna hurt you."

From the sound of Bobby's breathing, he was close. Mara willed herself to run faster. Fear coursed through her. Her chest felt like it was going to split open. Not seeing it in time, she ran full-throttle into a dirty metal garbage can but managed to right herself before she fell. The can tumbled over, spilling its contents onto the sidewalk. Bobby self-corrected too late and he tripped, taking a header over the can and onto the cement. Mara kept running, the sound of the prostitute's laughter fading with every step.

Several blocks later, Mara slowed to a walk and looked over her shoulder to make sure Bobby or the prostitute hadn't followed. No one came. She bent over and put her hands on her knees to catch her breath as tears welled in her eyes.

Stop it, Mara. You have to take care of yourself. There's nobody else to do it for you. She was used to taking care of the other foster kids back home. They were younger and looked up to her, like she was their big sister. Just once, Mara would've liked to have someone take care of her.

She wiped her eyes with the back of her arm and took a deep breath. The neighborhood looked less seedy than the one she'd just left. A couple of shops had colorful, pretty dresses in the window and she could smell spicy food cooking. She didn't notice any prostitutes hanging around and there were some nice older homes down the block with tidy yards. Mara walked into one of the dress shops, intending to ask for directions to the restaurant Keith told her about. She stood by the front counter and waited for the young woman to finish with her customer.

Mara liked the way the shop smelled; kind of sweet and smoky. A brass dish sat on the counter by the cash register with some dried leaves tied with pretty purple thread. A peace sign sticker in red and yellow and green had been affixed to the counter. She entertained herself by looking through the contents of another brass dish filled with beaded barrettes and hair ties.

The sales lady rang up the other woman's purchases and turned her attention to Mara.

"And what can I do for you, *cher*?" she said with a smile. Her accent had a lilting sound that Mara warmed to immediately.

"I think I'm lost. Can you please tell me where the Briar Cliff restaurant is? I'm supposed to meet somebody there and I got on the wrong bus." Mara hoped her little white lie was okay. She didn't want to go to hell, like her foster mother told her would happen.

"You surely did. The Briar Cliff is on the other side of town, near the beach." The woman arched her eyebrows. "Well, now, it looks like it's your lucky day, *cher*. I'm just about to close up shop and can drive you. Dis is no place for a little girl to be wanderin' around."

Mara's relief must have been evident, because the woman laughed as she opened the drawer to the register. "Would you do me a favor? See that sign in the window?" She pointed at a window by the entrance. "Can you turn it around so it says 'closed' to everybody outside?"

"Sure." Mara walked over to the door and turned the sign around. "Can I do anything else?"

"Look around the shop while I get tings in order." She glanced at Mara's filthy sundress. "Why don't you go and pick out someting from the clothes hangin' over there?" She indicated a sales rack on the far side of the shop. "We'll be ready to go before you know it."

"Anything?" Mara couldn't believe her good fortune when the woman nodded her head yes. She walked over to the rack and started to look through the clothes, picking out a sweater, a soft t-shirt and a pair of jeans. The jeans were a size too big for her, but she didn't care. Mara stepped into the changing room and pulled the heavy curtain closed.

The woman finished counting the till and started to shut off lights. "Are you coming, then?" She stood in the doorway leading to the back of the shop and waited.

"Yes." Mara got up from where she'd been sitting near the window and walked over to her, gripping the waistband of the jeans to keep them from sliding down her hips.

The woman leaned over and placed a thin leather belt in her hands. "I think you might need this." She straightened and smiled as she smoothed Mara's hair back. "You gonna be just fine, *cher.*"

CHAPTER NINETEEN

ILES AND JEAN WERE OUT BY the pool when Leine returned from her visit with Lou. She sent the temporary security guard on his way and walked out to join them. Jean appeared more relaxed than she had earlier. That in itself hit Leine as odd. Wouldn't a mother whose daughter was abducted be stressed out, pacing the floor, on the internet, searching for clues to her whereabouts? A pitcher of Miles' infamous tequila slushies rested on the table between them. Maybe she'd had a few too many. Leine hoped not. She didn't want to babysit the woman if she experienced a blackout. They both looked up as she approached.

Miles picked up the nearly empty pitcher to top off his glass. "Hey, Leine. You're back." He poured some in Jean's glass and set it on the table. "Jean and me were just talking about what we'll do when we get Mara back. I want them both to move in here. That way they'll always have a home, and I'll have a family."

Was he kidding? That boy was way too trusting. She'd have to deal with him later. "That's great, Miles. I need to speak to you, Jean." Leine took a seat next to her, noting her eyes had a wary look to them, like she'd heard it all before and disappointment tended to be the dominant outcome in her life.

Leine hesitated before continuing, unsure how she would react to what she was about to tell her. She looked directly into her eyes. "I just spoke with a friend of mine who works at a non-profit to end human trafficking."

Jean gripped her napkin and looked away, as if refusing to acknowledge what might come next. Leine reached over and touched her hand. She drew her gaze back to Leine's.

"He recently received information your daughter has run away from the traffickers and is out on the streets," Leine said.

Jean sat motionless for a moment, then rose from her chair and began to tear the napkin in her hand into little pieces. Leine watched as it floated to the ground like confetti.

"That's good news, right? We have to find her." Jean turned and looked at Leine, panic filling her eyes. "She can't be out there alone. So much could happen to her..." Jean sat down in her chair, then stood, as though unsure what to do next. "We have to go and get her..."

Leine reached out and laid her hand on Jean's, hoping her touch would calm her down. "Since Mara's no longer with the traffickers, we have a better chance of finding her, now. My friend sent word to his people on the street, so they're looking for her, but he suggested you contact the police. That could work, as long as she remains out of the trafficker's hands."

"Do you think the kidnappers know where she is?" Miles asked.

"Two men have been looking for her. One of them claims to be her uncle. He had an Eastern European accent," Leine said.

Jean closed her eyes, her shoulders sagging. "I can't go to the police. They told me I'd never see her again if I did." She sank into the chaise lounge and covered her face with her hands.

"They can't send her away if they don't physically have her, Jean. We need to find her first. The LAPD can help us with that." Leine wanted to take her by the shoulders and shake her, tell her to wake the hell up, but held back. There was no sense in upsetting her more.

Jean raised her head and looked at Leine, her eyes hardening. "No. I won't do that. What if they get to her first and know I talked to the cops? They'll send her away forever."

"She was never coming back, Jean." Leine took a deep breath to rein in her frustration. "I have to tell you in the strongest terms possible that I believe you are making a huge mistake. The more boots on the ground to search for her, the better chance we have of locating Mara before the traffickers do."

"She's right," Miles said. "More people will be able to find her sooner. Once we find her, we can start the new life we've been talking about."

Jean looked away without a reply. Leine pulled one of Lou's cards from her pocket. "I can see you're determined to do this the hard way. Take my friend's card. It's got his personal cell phone number and a twenty-four hour hotline. Call him anytime. He'll help you. He's a good man."

Jean accepted the card but laid it on the table. Leine didn't like the set of her jaw or the resolute look on her face. The traffickers must have done a number on her. Her refusal to get help didn't jibe with the way a worried mother would react when presented with a viable alternative. But, what did Leine know? Maybe Jean hadn't told them the whole story. Maybe they threatened to do more than she'd let on.

"Where did they see Mara last?" Jean asked.

"A homeless shelter downtown."

Jean leaned forward. "We should go there, then. That's within a few blocks of where you saw her at the theater, right? Knowing Mara, I think she'd try to stay in one place since she doesn't know the city." She looked at Miles. "She doesn't know anyone in L.A. She might try to get to you again. Do you have any public appearances planned in the next few days?"

"Just some talk-shows, entertainment stuff, but they're all shot in a studio. I don't have anything like what you're talking about until the premiere on Saturday." Miles glanced at Leine. "Jean's right. We should look for her. Time's running out."

"And just how do you think you're going to do that in the middle of L.A.? You're too recognizable," Leine said.

"I can go incognito." Miles jumped up from his chair, clearly taken with the idea. "I've got a closet full of costumes and makeup upstairs. I've even got fake chins and noses." He rubbed his hands together. "I'll dress like a homeless person. No one will recognize me."

"I don't think that's a good idea, Miles. We're trying to keep you safe from kidnappers, remember?"

"That's what I pay you for. To keep me safe." He tilted his head toward Jean. "And my sister, too."

"That's not what we agreed. I am responsible for you, and you only, Miles. No offense, Jean, but you don't get two for the price of one. It doesn't work that way."

Jean held up her hand. "I don't need—" she began.

"Jean is my sister, Leine. I'll double your fee, as long as you agree to guard her, too."

"Does that include finding her daughter? Because I didn't sign on for that, either." Leine could feel her blood pressure rise and was having a hard time resisting the urge to leave. *Calm down, Leine. Work this out. You don't want word of this to filter back to the bastards running the investigation on you.* She had to stay under the radar—not give them any more fuel for the fire.

"Please, Leine? We've got to do something. I can't just sit here and do nothing. It's my niece, for God's sake. What would you do if it were your family?" Miles looked at her, his eyes pleading.

She wanted to remind him that the results confirming their relationship hadn't come back from the lab yet, but let it go for the time being. "Fine. Double my fee. I'll take you into Hollywood. The costume better be good, or I won't risk it. No one can recognize you."

"Done," Miles said. Leine ignored his proffered hand.

"I want your word you will listen to me and if I tell you to do something, you'll do it, no questions asked." Leine sighed as she thought about the logistical nightmare of keeping track of Miles in costume in Hollywood. She eyed the pitcher, estimating he'd had approximately three drinks. Not too bad, if you compared it to what he usually ingested prior to an evening out.

"Absolutely, Leine." Miles turned to Jean. "You game?"

Jean looked relieved. "Yes, definitely. Let's go."

"We'll do this one time. If we don't have any luck, then I want Jean's promise she will contact the police."

"Yes, yes, yes! I promise. But we'll find her, I know it." Jean squeezed Leine's arm as she got up and headed toward the house.

Leine sighed as she pulled out her phone to call for the car. It wouldn't be any harder to track them both as long as they stayed together. Besides, she'd begun to think it might be even more important to keep an eye on Jean.

CHAPTER TWENTY

IT WAS HALF PAST SIX by the time they made it to Hollywood Boulevard. Miles told his driver to let them out a couple of blocks east to begin their search. Leine suggested they chart their progress on her phone, keeping track of where they'd been and where they intended to go next. Their first stop was the homeless shelter where Mara was seen last. Leine asked to speak with the director.

Heinrich Bauer greeted them at the front door. "I was just leaving for the day. You caught me at a good moment," he said, his smile weary. He eyed Miles, with his filthy hair and several layers of well-used clothes. He'd gone all out in authenticating his costume and was sporting a fake nose and colored contacts. Leine would never have recognized him if she saw him on the street.

"I'm sorry. It's been a long day. Are you looking for a bed?" Heinrich asked. "We're booked for the evening, but I can call another shelter to see if they have room…"

"No, thank you. I'm Leine Basso, a friend of Lou Stokes from SHEN." Leine offered her card, which Heinrich took. "We're looking for the little girl you filed a report about a couple of days ago. The one with unusual green eyes?"

Recognition lit his face. "Ah, yes. She was by herself. Apparently a runaway. Two men came in looking for her. One of them claimed to be her uncle, but I had my doubts."

"Why is that?" Leine asked.

"He had a Russian accent and she did not. And, they didn't even remotely resemble one another. It's merely a hunch, but he seemed less interested in her well-being than a relative would normally be. I'll tell you what I told them. If you're trying to find someone, you should get to know the homeless people down here." He glanced at Miles. "But, I see you've already done so."

"Has she been back?" Jean asked.

"This is her mother, Jean," Leine said, by way of introduction.

"I see." Heinrich inclined his head as he glanced at her through his bifocals. "Then I was correct in my assumption about them. I'm sorry. No, she has not. If she does, I will contact the police. I'm sure you understand. I filed a similar report with the Human Trafficking Unit the day after she was here, so they have what little information I could provide. Once they have her in custody, they'll be able to sort this all out and return her to those who truly care for her. You've filed a report, of course."

Leine nodded. It served no purpose to put Jean on the spot, so she let his comment go. "That would be the best course of action, Mr. Bauer. Thank you for your time. If you hear anything about her being picked up by law enforcement, could you please give me a call?" She indicated the card in his hand. Heinrich squinted at it and nodded.

"Of course. I hope someone finds her soon. Twelve years old on these streets is like a young gazelle loose in a field of hungry lions."

Leine glanced at Jean, but it was hard to gauge her reaction. "Again, Mr. Bauer, thank you for your time." They walked him to his car in the parking lot behind the building and watched him drive away.

"Well that was a waste of time." Jean said, pacing back and forth. "Except now we know how the kidnappers found out about Mara being at the shelter. Just like they said, they have someone in the LAPD."

"Not necessarily."

Jean gave Leine a look. "Right. The guy submits a report to the cops and the two kidnappers just happen to check this homeless shelter two days later? Come on, Leine. You can't be serious." Jean closed her eyes and leaned against the wall.

"They could have come up with the idea of checking shelters the same way we did. It's not rocket science." Leine watched Jean with acute interest. What was it about the police that had her so worried? The background check hadn't turned up any major criminal activity. She made a mental note to run a more thorough investigation when they got back. "Either way, if she does show up again and he calls the cops, no one's going to be able to take her from a police station except her legal guardian."

"I'm sorry. You're right. It's just that I don't know what to think. I'm so scared of what they'll do. He led me to believe they have a long reach," Jean said.

Leine noted the sagging skin around her eyes. She looked exhausted.

"Well, are we going to keep looking? I didn't get all gussied up to stand here and look pretty." Miles smiled, his teeth exceedingly white against his dirty face.

"You might not want to smile too often," Leine said, and tapped her finger against her teeth.

Miles caught her meaning and groaned. "Shit. How stupid is that to forget to yellow my teeth?"

"You could always chew on some dirt. There's plenty of it available," Leine suggested.

"Uh-huh. Did I tell you there was a limit to my realism? Let's go. We're not doing Mara any good here."

They walked back to Hollywood Boulevard and headed toward Grauman's Chinese Theater. Traffic was heavy. Leine glanced to her right in time to see a black 1969 Camaro SS drive past, Santiago Jensen in the driver's seat. Leine's heart stopped when she realized he wasn't alone. The distinct silhouette of a woman's head with long, flowing hair could be seen sitting in the passenger side. Leine watched as the taillights melted into the others, disappearing with the rest of the traffic.

He could be giving someone a ride home, Leine argued with herself. It was the end of the day and Jensen would probably offer a ride, especially to a woman. Still, Leine felt a twinge of possessiveness rear its ugly head. *You have no hold on him, Leine. He's a free agent and can be with whomever he chooses, the same as you.* Her pep talk didn't do much for the way she was feeling. Miles nudged her with his elbow.

"You all right? You look like you want to rip somebody's head off," he said.

"I'm fine." Leine made an effort to smile. She could tell by the way Miles looked at her that it wasn't working. "Really, Miles. Nothing's wrong."

Miles did an eye-roll. They continued to the forecourt of Grauman's Theater to join the crowd of tourists and cartoon characters, and hopefully find Mara.

Ned and Yuri walked across the alley, headed toward the Gospel Mission Homeless Center. Ned had suggested they continue to work Heinrich Bauer as a contact, arguing that he was plugged into the homeless community and would hear about Mara before they'd even gotten a hint of where she was. Yuri was about ready to snuff helpful Ned and dump his body off the Santa Monica Pier. Finding Mara was Yuri's responsibility, not Ned's.

"Did you ever call Fournier's publicist to find out where his next appearance will be?" Ned asked. Yuri rolled his eyes.

"Yes, I called her. He doesn't have anything scheduled for the general public until the premiere of his latest movie."

"When's that?"

"Not until Saturday."

Ned groaned. "Christ. Greg's going to have our asses in a sling way before then."

Yuri nodded, a glum look on his face.

"What if we don't find her?" Ned asked.

"I don't want to think about it." For starters, Greg would be in trouble with the big client, could even end up losing his business. It didn't matter to Yuri. He'd be one dead Ukrainian before then. His feet hurt from pounding the pavement for fourteen hours a day. The closest they'd gotten to finding Mara was when they beat the hell out of that cowardly little cartoon character after he brought them to his run-down apartment. Yuri was certain she would be there by the way the little man was acting. But, somehow she'd slipped away, and he hadn't seen or heard of her since. He didn't dare go back to Greg without her, and hadn't called in for two days.

They turned the corner before the shelter and Yuri stopped in his tracks. Unaware he'd stopped, Ned nearly ran him over.

"What?" Ned followed Yuri's gaze.

Four people stood on the sidewalk outside the homeless shelter: Bauer, a homeless bum and two women. The women seemed familiar, but were turned away from them, so he wasn't sure where he knew them from. One of the them turned and Yuri got a glimpse of her in profile. She was the tall brunette Yuri'd seen at Grauman's the other day. That clinched it. Now he remembered where he'd seen her before.

"Do you recognize the woman with Bauer?" Yuri asked Ned.

Ned shook his head. "No, should I?"

"If you want to get in good with my people, yes."

"Okay." Ned waited a minute then said, "Well? Are you going to tell me?"

Yuri leaned down next to Ned's ear and lowered his voice. "That, my friend, is the woman who stole a precious artifact from Nadja Imports in West Hollywood a few months back, and killed my cousin Borys in the process. My uncle is so pissed off, he doesn't know whether to kill her or buy her a drink."

Ned gave Yuri a sidelong glance. "If she stole something precious and killed a relative, why would you buy her a drink? That makes no sense."

"It is rumored that many years ago she killed the one called the Frenchman. An enemy so reviled, anyone who exterminated that rat-fuck would go down in Russian history as a saint."

"Then it was okay that she stole whatever it was. I get it." Ned nodded his head knowingly.

Yuri spat on the ground. "No. What she stole was part of the Frenchman's heritage. My uncle kept it displayed above his desk. It belonged to those the Frenchman wronged."

"Okay. Then you should kill her or try to get the artifact back, right?" Ned cocked his head, frowning.

Yuri shook his head. "Impossible. The artifact is gone, taken by police during an investigation of the rat-fuck's son. That woman was in league with the Frenchman's descendant."

"But why would she help the Frenchman's son if she killed the father? Some twisted sense of responsibility?" Ned rubbed his temples. "You're sure it's her?"

"I am certain. We must follow her, find out where she lives."

"We can't, Yuri. We have to find the girl, remember?"

"No. This comes before anything else."

"Even your life? Because that's what's gonna happen if we don't find her." Ned raised his eyebrows.

"Yes. Even my life. Family is everything. I would never forgive myself if I did nothing with this opportunity. It is given from God. I'm certain of it. I, Yuri Kovshevnikov, must follow the woman assassin and report back to my uncle. He will decide what to do with the information."

Chapter Twenty-One

THE LIGHTS SURROUNDING THE THEATER'S forecourt gave the area a festive air, drawing tourists like slugs to spilled beer. Leine and Jean stayed a couple of feet behind Miles, who earned a disgusted stare or two from onlookers. To Leine's surprise, a few of the tourists offered him money, which Miles took, arguing he had to in order to stay in character. One younger guy in a green t-shirt even handed him a hotdog he'd just bought.

He insisted on interviewing the cartoon characters to see if any of them had seen Mara. Leine wasn't optimistic that the questions would lead anywhere. She assumed the two men looking for her had already done so, and she wasn't sure how forceful they'd been in their questioning. Either way, it would inevitably make the characters more wary of strangers. Jean remained on the sidelines and kept quiet, letting Miles do the talking.

Miles walked over to someone in a Darth Vader costume who was between tourists and tapped him on the shoulder. Darth Vader turned and breathed heavily, doing a fair imitation of the overlord. "What do you want, earthling?"

Miles took out the picture of Mara. "Have you seen this little girl anywhere?"

Darth leaned in to get a closer look and shook his helmeted head. "No, earthling. I have not." He pointed at a white pantyhose-legged SpongeBob Square Pants who stood in the corner at the far end of the courtyard of the theater, having his picture taken with a well-fed family of six. "You might try speaking with that sponge-creature over there. He tends to be the best connected of us."

"Thanks." Miles smiled. Darth Vader straightened and took a step back.

"You look familiar to me, earth dweller. How do I know you?"

Miles pulled out a twenty dollar bill from within the folds of his crusty jacket and handed it to him. "You don't."

"As you wish." Darth Vader bowed as he palmed the twenty and walked away.

"I told you not to smile, Miles. It's a dead giveaway," Leine said as they headed toward SpongeBob.

"Yeah, I know. I fucked up. But at least we got a lead, right?" Miles started to smile but stopped himself.

Leine signaled Jean and they fell back a few steps as Miles waited for SpongeBob to finish up with his group of pudgy tourists. She figured he'd talk more openly to a street person.

She was wrong.

SpongeBob took a swipe at Miles with his cartoon hand. "Get the hell away from me, you dirty-ass son-of-a-bitch. You're fucking with my business."

In seconds, Leine was behind him, her gun jammed into the foam back of his costume. She leaned down and whispered in his ear. "This is a nine-millimeter Glock. You will lower your voice and do exactly as I say, yes?"

SpongeBob nodded.

"Good. Now this gentleman just wants to ask you a couple of questions. We can do it here, or we can do it somewhere more...private."

"Here works," SpongeBob replied, his voice a squeak.

"Fine. Go ahead." She wrinkled her nose. The guy's costume was ripe.

Miles stopped staring at Leine and cleared his throat. Then he showed him Mara's picture. "Have you seen this little girl?"

SpongeBob shook his head. "Like I told the other two thugs, I never seen her, but the other SpongeBob did."

"Where can we find him?" Miles asked.

SpongeBob hesitated. Leine pressed the barrel of the gun into his back. The Godfather's theme song erupted from the phone in her pocket. She didn't answer.

"I heard someone say he's in County General. He got beat up real bad." SpongeBob's voice trailed off.

Leine could feel him start to shake. The little shit probably had something to do with it. "And why would that be, Bob?"

SpongeBob shrugged. "I don't know."

With a sigh, Leine wrenched his arm back at an unnatural angle and held it there. "Why is he in County General, Bob?" she asked again.

"I...I think it was the two guys looking for your little girl. They beat the shit out of him. That's it. That's all I know."

"What's his name?"

"Keith something."

Leine let go of his arm and pulled back the Glock's slide for effect.

"Keith Price," SpongeBob sputtered. The distinct odor of urine assaulted Leine's nose. She took a step backward as she holstered her gun.

"Looks like we're going to County General," Leine said.

Chapter Twenty-Two

KEITH PRICE SHARED A ROOM WITH three other patients. Hooked up to oxygen and two IVs, his face was a bruised mess, with one eye swollen shut. He wore a sling on one arm and both legs were out of the covers, encased in casts. Even his toes looked bruised.

Jean stood in the hallway at the request of the floor nurse as Leine walked around the side of the hospital bed. Miles waited in the lobby downstairs, having been stopped by security at the door for his attire.

Keith appeared peaceful in repose, although Leine imagined he'd been given some serious pain killers. The boy was a mess. His breathing was deep and even, though, and the nurse had assured her he'd recover, albeit with a few more scars than before.

Leine was told she could visit with Keith for a brief time, but not to tax him. She pushed on the mattress, reluctant to touch him. He snorted, once, and opened his good eye.

"Hi Keith. My name is Leine Basso." Leine produced the photo and turned it toward him. "I'm sorry to bother you. I realize you must be in a lot of pain, but I need to find this little girl." He blinked. "I understand you incurred these injuries from two men who were also looking for her."

Keith blinked again. His eye watered.

"I realize you want to keep her safe. I do, too. The two men who put you in the hospital work for sex traffickers. Our latest information is that she's still at large. They haven't found her yet." Keith closed his good eye and swallowed. Leine continued. "I'm working with her mother who is desperate to find her." She nodded toward Jean. "Any information you can give us will at least put us on a par with the bad guys."

"That's her mom?" Keith's voice came out in a croak.

"Yes. Do you want me to get her?"

Keith shook his head, once. He grimaced.

"She was staying with me. I told the two…men. But she wasn't there when we went to my apartment." He paused for a moment, then continued. "I didn't tell them where she was going."

Leine leaned in close to hear him. He was weak, his voice hardly above a whisper.

"She thinks Miles Fournier is going to help her. I found out where his favorite restaurant is and gave her the address. She's going to go there every night until he shows up and she can talk to him."

"What's the name of the restaurant?"

"Briar Cliff." Keith closed his eye again, his breathing heavy from the strain of speaking.

"Thanks, Keith. You've been a big help."

"She's a sweet girl. I hope you find her."

Keith's breathing became deep and more even, indicating he'd fallen into the sleep of the heavily medicated. Leine walked over to the drawer with his name on it and slid it open. Inside, folded neatly, she found a pair of jeans and a t-shirt covered in dried blood. She took out a business card and scribbled a note on the back, then slipped three hundreds along with the card into the front pocket of the jeans before she shut the drawer.

Leine and Jean emerged from the elevator into the lobby, looking for Miles. They spotted him sitting outside the front entrance on a cement bench. Jean excused herself to go to the ladies room.

"Well?" Miles asked as Leine sat down next to him.

"Good call. I found out Mara's trying to get to you for help. Keith somehow found out your favorite restaurant and gave her the address. He didn't tell the two goons who beat him up. That gives us a little head start."

"Which favorite restaurant? I've got a few."

"The Briar Cliff."

Miles looked surprised. "The Briar Cliff? Geez, I haven't been there in ages. I used to go every Thursday for their prime rib, but it got old after a while." He shook his head. "God, if we didn't find Keith, how would we ever have known she was waiting for me there?"

"Sometimes the gods smile on the good guys, Miles."

"Well, looks like we're going out for prime rib, eh?"

"Prime rib? What are you guys talking about?" Jean appeared behind them.

Leine slid over on the bench to make room. "The favorite restaurant of Miles' Keith told me about. Or, at least what used to be his favorite restaurant. That's what he used to order."

Jean's face lit up. "Let's go."

Leine glanced at her watch. "Too late now. The kitchen's probably closed for the night. We'll try tomorrow."

118

"Yeah and besides, they wouldn't let me in the building dressed like this." Miles laughed. "Hey, Jean, we're close to finding Mara. Isn't that great?"

Jean smiled, relief obvious on her face. "That's more than great, Miles. That's the best news I've heard all week."

Leine noticed Jean's smile didn't quite reach her eyes. She wondered if she was just tired from the search, or if there was another reason.

CHAPTER TWENTY-THREE

ANTIAGO JENSEN THREW HIS KEYS in the dish on the hall table and kicked the door shut with his foot. Loosening his tie, he thumbed through the mail, but didn't find anything that needed his immediate attention. He walked to the kitchen and grabbed a bottle of Scotch from the cupboard, poured three fingers into a glass and dropped in a few ice cubes.

Drink in hand, he returned to the living room and flicked on the television with the remote. Soccer. Usually something he liked to watch in order to wind down at the end of the day, but not today. He stared at the screen, not seeing anything as his mind ran through what he'd found out earlier that afternoon.

In the spirit of improved relations between the LAPD and the FBI, the feds had offered new information on the Leine Basso investigation. The latest showed Leine in L.A. at the time of the murders. Airline manifests, bank accounts and car rental agreements listed the aliases she supposedly used within the agency. The information was too pat, too perfect. The whole 'rogue agent' BS didn't sit well with either him or Putz.

Jensen realized it wouldn't matter if Leine was innocent or not. It was clear the Agency expected her to take the fall for the murders.

He tipped his head and threw back the Scotch in one swallow. Leine was being set up, he could feel it. But how the hell could he prove that she didn't commit the murders? She'd been an assassin, for Christ's sake. Pretty hard to argue that point, since she'd even admitted it to Jensen. He could see their reasoning: why not have LAPD pin the charges on an outlier, someone who was no longer with the Agency? But Jensen wouldn't let a person who didn't commit the murders pay the ultimate price. Not on his watch.

Especially not Leine.

The only way forward Jensen could see was to ask Leine for the files she claimed she'd sent to Eric's boss at the Agency. For her sake, he hoped she had copies. He'd have to be careful who he gave them to and when. Jensen had a couple of contacts in the FBI that he trusted, but was pretty sure being in possession of the files would not be good for their careers. There's no way faster onto a fibbie's shit-list than to screw with their career trajectory. And, if what Leine said about her ex-boss was true, it could be dangerous.

Jensen massaged the space between his eyes. He had to call her. There was no other way. He could've had Putz call, but didn't want to involve his partner. The less he knew, the better. He stared at the disposable phone he'd bought earlier that day after he found out the latest developments in the case. He'd even checked to make sure the store didn't have surveillance cameras directed at the front counter, and wore a pair of sunglasses and a ball cap to hide his features.

When the hell did he start acting like the people he took off the streets?

Leine Basso had a hold on him he couldn't shake. He thought about her when he was awake and dreamed about her at night. His only respite came when he was one-on-one with a suspect or deep into working a case. Even then, memories of the first day they met at the reality show's studio to their last encounter at his apartment floated to the surface of his brain with a force he couldn't ignore. Everything about her—the smell of her perfume, the way her eyes looked after they'd made love, how her body felt in his hands, her smile—had been seared into his memory and stoked a fire he couldn't begin to know how to contain.

Maybe he didn't want to.

Admit it, Santa. You're on the hook. This was new territory for Santiago Jensen, Babe-Magnet Extraordinaire, or BME, as his partner referred to him. He'd always wondered how perfectly good cops could throw everything away, just for a taste. Now he knew. And this connection between them went far deeper than sex.

He knew his belief in Leine's innocence wasn't entirely because of his attraction to her, however. Putz had the same gut feeling, which confirmed it for Jensen.

He picked up the phone and dialed Leine's number.

CHAPTER TWENTY-FOUR

THE MAÎTRE' D AT THE BRIAR Cliff seated Miles, Jean, April, and Leine at a table by a window. The low lighting, mahogany tables, and rich leather chairs conjured exclusivity and power. Leine sat next to the window. She'd already checked outside the building, but found nothing indicating Mara's presence.

"Thanks, Jonathan. Is Chef Mark working tonight?" Miles asked as he accepted a menu.

"He is. Would you like me to ask him to come to the front of the house, Mr. Fournier?" Jonathan replied with a smile.

"If he's not too busy."

April giggled as Miles winked at her.

Jonathan continued his fawning. "May I say how wonderful it is to see you again? We've missed your visits."

"You're too kind. I've been so wrapped up with promotion for the movie and all."

"Of course. I understand. Would you care to start off with a bottle of cabernet?"

"Absolutely. Four glasses."

"A carafe of water, please," Leine added.

Jonathan gave a quick nod and disappeared into the kitchen in a flurry of efficiency. April leaned over to whisper in Miles' ear and giggled again.

Leine had voiced her objections to Miles including April since they were there to make contact with Mara and bring her home. She wasn't sure how much the Russians knew and was loathe to put her daughter in harm's way. April had pleaded with her to let her come along and Leine allowed herself to be talked into it, grudgingly. She was still a pansy-ass when it came to her daughter.

April fished her phone from her purse to answer a text message and Jean excused herself from the table. Leine watched her leave. She turned back to Miles and said in a low voice that April wasn't able to hear, "My contact at DNAsty Labs called earlier. The results of the DNA testing will be available the day after tomorrow." Zephyr had left a hurried message on Leine's phone, telling her he'd email her the report as soon as it was available.

Miles frowned. "I'd forgotten about that."

"What will you do if the results are different than you—"

"I don't want to talk about it, Leine. We'll deal with that when and if we have to." His face brightened. "Ah…here we are," he said as Jonathan returned to the table with the bottle of wine and glasses.

Leine glanced at the hallway near the bathrooms to make sure Jean wasn't within earshot and caught a glimpse of her talking on a cell phone. She'd never seen her use one before. In fact, she hadn't realized Jean even owned a cell phone.

"I'll be right back," Leine said to Miles. She rose from the table and headed to where Jean had been standing a second before. April didn't look up from her texting.

"Yes. We're at the Briar Cliff now—" Jean stopped talking when she saw Leine round the corner. She smiled at her and continued. "I need to hang up now. I think we're ready to order. I'll call you after dinner, okay?" She hit the end button and put the phone in her purse. "Am I holding up dinner?"

"No, not at all. Jonathan just brought the wine. I'm headed to the ladies room," Leine replied. "If you don't mind my asking, who were you just talking to?"

"My friend back in Nevada. She's worried about Mara and wants me to update her whenever there's a new development. And—" Jean rolled her eyes, "—she's a little star-struck that I'm hanging out with Miles." She smiled sheepishly. "Sometimes I have to pinch myself, too. I mean, my brother is Miles Fournier. Wow." She shook her head as though she couldn't quite believe it.

"I'll bet." Leine smiled. "Meet you back at the table in a minute." She slipped into the bathroom and waited a few moments before returning to her seat.

The prime rib Miles had ordered looked good, but the grilled fish was even better. April and Miles seemed to be getting along well, trading snarky remarks about the other patrons, but the conversation between the four of them had a deeper undertone that underscored the reason they were all there. April's phone played the tone Leine recognized as the one she'd selected for Cory.

"Sorry. I'd better take this." Her face bright pink, April walked out to the foyer to answer the call.

Leine took a sip of wine and was ready to dig into her fingerling potatoes when Jean excused herself again. Leine watched her actually walk into the bathroom this time. She turned back to her meal, but noticed Miles looking at her, a scowl on his face.

"What? You don't like the way I'm eating?" she asked.

"You never let up, do you? You're going to be surprised when the DNA test shows she's my sister." He pushed a stalk of asparagus around on his plate with his fork. "Can't you let things rest? Jean tells me she feels like you're watching her every move. Like you don't trust her."

"I don't. That's what you're paying me for, Miles. To watch out for you and keep you safe. In order to do that, I can't allow myself to trust anyone."

"Even me?"

"Even you. Look. I agreed to take on Jean's protection as part of my job, but if the DNA results are negative, I'm going to have a hard time justifying the change in my job description."

"Meaning—"

"Meaning if that happens and you allow her to remain in your home, I'll have no choice but to resign."

"She's my sister. I'm sure of it."

"I hope you're right."

Leine's attention shifted to movement in the shadows near the well-tended hedge outside the window. A young, dark-haired girl stood just outside the landscape lights.

Mara.

Mara's eyes widened, obviously recognizing Miles seated at the table. She ran forward and pounded on the window.

"Mr. Fournier—" she cried, her words muffled by the thickness of the glass. Miles dropped his fork and started to get up.

Leine was out of her seat in an instant, intending to move outside and coax her in, but a look of fear crossed the young girl's features. Her complexion turned white as she backed away from the window. Then she turned and ran.

A moment later, Jean appeared at the table, her face a mixture of hope and confusion.

"Mara?" she asked.

"Had to be," Leine replied, throwing her napkin on the table. "I'm going after her." She ran through the dining room into the foyer past April and was out the main door in seconds. She sprinted around the front of the building to the window, but Mara wasn't there. A car door closed behind her. She turned in time to see a sleek black BMW pull away from the curb and race out of the parking lot. Inside, the driver's silhouette was barely visible through the smoked glass window. She noted the license plate number, then quickly scouted the perimeter of the restaurant. She found no sign of Mara. Had she been in the car? When she returned to the front of the restaurant, the other three stood in the doorway, waiting for her.

"She's gone?" Miles asked.

Leine nodded her head, her frustration rising from having been so close to rescuing Mara.

"God, she's so *young*." Miles closed his eyes as if trying to erase the picture of Mara's face.

Jean put her napkin to her mouth as she ran inside the restaurant.

"Jean thinks it was you, Leine." Miles turned to face her, his arms crossed. "She thinks Mara freaked when you got out of your chair. That she saw the gun."

"She wasn't even looking at me when she bolted," Leine snapped. "How does Jean know what she was doing? I thought she was in the bathroom."

"She says she saw the whole thing."

"Then why did she ask me if it was Mara? Wouldn't she recognize her own daughter?"

"She says it was too far to see clearly."

April looked from Miles to her mother. "I'm confused. Why would she be scared of my mother?"

"Apparently, Mara's deathly afraid of guns. It's possible that when Leine got up from the table that she saw the one Leine was wearing and got scared."

Leine glanced at her clothing. She doubted her jacket would have opened enough for Mara to spot the weapon. "Kind of odd Jean's not out here looking for her daughter, don't you think?"

Miles leaned his head back and sighed. "Christ, Leine. Can't you give the woman a break? We almost got her daughter back, but now you—or something—scared her off. Obviously, she doesn't want to talk to you. She's really upset."

"Stop it, both of you," April said, putting her hand on Leine's arm.

"Where the hell did she go?" Leine shook off her daughter's hand and brushed past Miles into the restaurant, scanning the room for Jean. She wasn't in the dining area. Leine strode to the ladies room and pushed open the door. Jean was on her cell again. This time she didn't say goodbye to whomever she was talking to and slipped the phone inside her purse.

"What do you want?" Jean's mouth was set in a grim line. Anger radiated off of her.

Without thinking, Leine ripped the nine millimeter from its holster and pointed it at her. "Who were you talking to just now?"

Jean's face paled as she stared at Leine. "I told you. A...a friend from Nevada—" Beads of sweat rolled down her face. She started to shake.

Keeping the gun on her, Leine reached inside Jean's purse and pulled out her phone.

"You can't do that," Jean hissed.

Leine lowered the gun and stepped back as she pressed the icon for recent calls. The air snapped between them. She'd barely caught a glimpse of the last number called when Jean lunged forward and smacked the phone from her hand. Bits of plastic scattered as it hit the floor.

Leine narrowed her eyes. "Nevada? I don't think so, Jean. The number's local."

"Where the hell do you get off?" Jean ran to the cell and stepped on the case, grinding it into the tile. She looked back at Leine, tears streaming down her face. "Fuck you," she said, and stormed out of the bathroom.

Leine slid her gun back into the holster and bent over to examine the phone. It didn't look salvageable. Taking a moment to compose herself, she pocketed the larger pieces before she walked out to join the others.

April stood in the hallway near the kitchen, talking to a man dressed in whites and a chef's hat. Jean and Miles were in the foyer, speaking in hushed tones. Jean abruptly stopped talking and they both turned as she approached.

"What the hell are you doing?" Miles demanded, his eyes dark with anger. "Jean says you threatened her." He nodded toward the bathroom. "With a *gun*."

"Miles, you need to listen to me—"

Miles held up his hand. "No—" He rounded on her. "You need to listen. You work for me, remember?"

"She's lying to you."

Jean put her hand on his arm and shook her head. "She's crazy, Miles. No wonder she scared Mara."

Leine sighed in disgust. "She said she was calling a friend in Nevada, but it was a local number."

"That's a lie, Miles. I did no such thing."

"Let's get this over with, once and for all," Miles said. He held out his hand. "Give me your phone, Jean."

"I can't," Jean answered as fresh tears fell. "I dropped it when Leine attacked me and it broke."

"For your information, she hit it out of my hand and then stepped on it so the number can't be recovered. How convenient, eh, Jean?"

"That's a lie." Jean practically spat the words.

Leine crossed her arms. "Who are you going to believe? Which one of us has the most to lose here?"

Miles looked from Jean back to Leine, confusion evident on his face.

"Look, Miles. For some reason, Mara got spooked tonight. I was there by the window when she tried to get your attention, remember? It wasn't me she's afraid of, and I doubt she saw the gun. There's one other possibility: it might have had something to do with the black car I saw speeding out of the parking lot."

Jean and Miles both stared at her. "What black car?" Miles asked, obviously alarmed.

"A black sedan pulled out as I came around front. I didn't get a good look at the driver, but I memorized the plates."

Miles stiffened. "You think someone got her? Jesus." He rubbed his hand over his eyes.

"I didn't say that. I said I saw a black sedan speeding off, not that I saw her inside the car. It's a possibility we have to consider."

"Oh, God," Jean said, and slid down the wall to the floor.

Miles dropped to a crouch and wrapped his arm around Jean's shoulder. He glanced up at Leine. "If she wasn't in the car and you or your gun scared her off, there's no way she'll come near me. Not as long as you're around. And, if they got her, then we're back to square one." His expression hardened. "It's not only because of Mara. You pulled a gun on my *sister*, Leine. I have to let you go."

April inhaled sharply, but didn't say anything. Jean's expression held a mixture of relief and something else Leine couldn't quite pinpoint. Triumph?

"Do you really think—"

"You can stay the night, then pack your things tomorrow. I'll call for your replacement in the morning."

Leine checked at the finality in his tone. Summoning her self-control, she gave him a quick nod. "Fine. If that's what you want, I won't argue. It's your call. I think you're making a huge mistake, Miles."

Jean leaned her head on Miles' chest and he wrapped his arm more tightly around her shoulders. "You're wrong, Leine. Jean's right about this. She knows her own daughter."

Leine stopped a valet passing by and asked him to bring the car around. "You'd sure think so, wouldn't you?"

131

CHAPTER TWENTY-FIVE

FROM THE DEEP SHADOW OF a small stand of wind-swept pines, Mara watched the black car leave the parking lot. Tears streamed down her face as she fought the hopelessness that threatened to engulf her. *Why was that woman with Miles?* Now she had no one to turn to. Miles wouldn't help her, not when he was obviously friends with the dark-haired lady.

Mara slid down the trunk of the tree to sit, ignoring the rough bark that scraped her back and wondered what to do next. This had been her big chance to get the actor to help her. The nice woman from the dress shop had given her a telephone number to call in case no one came to get her, but Mara was afraid she would report her to the cops, and they'd for sure send her back to the foster monster's house. Miles would understand. He was raised in foster care, too.

Weariness flowed through her body. She couldn't think straight, she was so tired. Tempted to fall asleep right there, she thought better of the idea and stood up.

She walked through the trees and down an embankment to a cleared spot on a ridge above the ocean where she'd slept the night before. The sound of the waves pounding against the shore soothed her as she gazed at the starlit sky. It was cooler here at night than in the city, but Mara didn't mind. She loved the ocean, had never seen it before coming to California. She'd spent the daylight hours waiting for Miles to show up walking along the beach, picking up shells and pretty rocks, and watching the birds. The half-eaten food in the garbage bin behind the restaurant hadn't been so bad. She was grateful to the woman in the dress shop for giving her new clothes to wear. The jeans and sweater kept her warm at night, and she looked normal, not all dirty.

Mara's thoughts turned back to the black car in the parking lot. Could it have been the men who were looking for her? She didn't want to find out and hid so the man driving the car couldn't see her. So many people were looking for her, but she only wanted to be found by one person. Miles Fournier. Mara sighed as she watched a satellite float across the night sky. One of the kids at her foster home had showed her how to spot them, and now she always looked.

Maybe he won't bring the woman with him next time. If he did, she was going to have to think of another plan.

CHAPTER TWENTY-SIX

THE ELEVATOR DOOR PINGED OPEN and Leine stepped into the familiar hallway. Jensen had called and left a message asking her to stop by when she had a chance. She didn't recognize the phone number. Contacting a person who was under investigation for three murders wasn't a good career move for a homicide detective.

She couldn't shake the dark cloud hanging above her head since Miles let her go, and it continued to dog her to Jensen's apartment. This couldn't be good news. Jensen's tone hadn't been what she'd call friendly.

She reached his apartment door and knocked. She wore a low-cut, feminine blouse and tight-fitting skirt that showed off her legs, sans underwear. There wasn't any reason they couldn't say a proper hello to each other first.

The lock slid free and the door opened. The instant Leine and Jensen's eyes met, a bolt of electricity shot through her, curling her toes. The same reaction she always had when he looked at her. Judging by his expression, he felt the same. Jensen managed a smile and stepped aside as she walked into his apartment. Leine scanned the room for traces of another woman, but found none. *Maybe he really did just give someone a ride home.*

"Leine." He walked behind her to close the door and brushed her arm.

"Santa." Leine turned to him as she placed her purse on the hall table. She moved in for a kiss, but he stepped back and shook his head.

"No, Leine. What I have to tell you—"

Leine placed her finger across his lips and slid her hand up his chest. His breathing quickened as she began to unbutton his shirt. At the same time she gently kissed him and nipped at his neck, feeling her blood warm, losing herself in his scent. She trailed her other hand along his hip and curved inward.

With a groan, Jensen buried his face in her hair, inhaling deeply. His hands dropped to the hem of her skirt and he slid it upward. At that moment, Leine forgot the reason she was there, wanting only to feel him again. Nothing else mattered; the place could go up in flames and she wouldn't care.

Jensen moved her back until she was against the wall. His hands caressed her hips and then moved down to her ass. Leine slid her leg along his thigh, hooked it behind him and pulled him closer. Her breathing matched his as he lifted her off her feet. She wrapped her legs around his waist while he shrugged free of his jeans, and leaned her head back with a sigh.

Jensen finished dressing and helped Leine smooth her skirt. Her lips were swollen where he'd kissed her, and he lightly brushed his thumb over them. He wanted to tell her how much he loved her, but couldn't bring himself to say the words. The news he had to deliver wasn't good, and he worried the end result would mean she'd be gone from his life forever. The fact that he loved her wouldn't change anything.

Leine smiled and kissed his fingers, her eyes a sleepy version of the ones he always dreamed about. He refused to ask why this was happening. The first time Santiago Jensen found himself deeply in love and it was with someone who had a past like Leine's. Once he told her what the feds were up to, it would only be a matter of time before she disappeared.

"How's the security detail going? Glamorous, right?" He'd avoided reading anything about Miles Fournier in case there was mention of his attractive female bodyguard.

Leine walked into the living room and took a seat on the couch. "It's gotten interesting. I'd like to talk to you about a recent development."

"Oh?" Jensen sat beside her and put his hand on her leg. She slid her hand in his and settled back. It felt natural, her being in his apartment, talking with her about her work. "What happened?" he asked, happy to delay the inevitable conversation.

"First of all, I'm no longer employed by Miles Fournier."

"Oh?"

"Long story. I'll get to it in a minute. A while ago a woman contacted him, claiming to be his sister."

"Easy enough to check."

She nodded. "I have samples at a lab and should be getting the results tomorrow. That's only part of the development. The woman is looking for her twelve-year-old daughter who was supposedly abducted by sex traffickers. We found out that she got away and was on her own on the streets."

"Was?"

"It's possible the traffickers found her. But I'm getting ahead of myself."

"Have you called the LAPD?"

"No. That's the weird part. The mother told me the traffickers said they have a mole in the department and would know if she reported her daughter was kidnapped. I could understand why she was reticent about contacting you guys when they had her, but now that the girl's supposedly out in the open, I don't see why she wouldn't want all hands on deck looking for her. It doesn't jibe. She has to be hiding something."

"Do you have any leads? Unless they've got her, it won't be long before someone else picks her up, either for sex or worse."

"We talked to a guy who had the crap beat out of him by two men who were looking for her. He said the girl believed Miles would help her if she could get to him, so he gave her the address of a restaurant that Miles supposedly frequented. She was going to hang out and wait for him to show up. We went there last night and she showed, but got scared and ran. That's where I think she may have been picked up."

"What spooked her?"

Leine shifted on the couch. "That's where it gets even weirder. Miles and Jean, the mother, are both convinced the kid was afraid of me, or, more specifically, my gun. Miles is so vested in helping this woman and her child that he canned me rather than risk the possibility of scaring her off again." She opted not to tell him about pulling the gun on Jean in the bathroom. Not her finest moment.

"Why would the kid be afraid of your gun? Did she see it?"

"I'm fairly certain she didn't. I think she ran either because she saw one of the traffickers or because she saw Jean. Those are the only logical explanations. And, Jean lied to me about a phone number she called, even went so far as to destroy her phone. I have a bad feeling about her, Santa. I don't think she's who she says she is. "

"The DNA results will tell you that."

"I just hope Miles listens if the test comes back negative."

"I'll report the girl to our Human Trafficking Unit. I seriously doubt they have a mole in the department. You can bet they told her that to get her to cooperate."

"The director of the Gospel Mission Homeless Center, Heinrich Bauer, said he filed a report with the unit, so maybe if you could flag it for them, let them know there's someone out there looking for her."

"Sure. Give me her description and I'll get it to them tomorrow."

"They need to be discreet. If Jean sees the police, I don't know how she'll react. It could put Miles in danger."

"But you said the traffickers might already have her?"

"When I ran out to the parking lot to find her, a black four-door BMW sped away. I didn't get a good look at the driver and I didn't see the girl, but I memorized the license plate."

"I'll run the number, see if it turns up anything."

"Thanks, Santa. I appreciate it. I've also got contacts I haven't reached out to yet who may be able to help."

"Why do you care so much about what happens to this girl?"

"She's got no one. Her own mother is afraid to get the police involved. The least I can do is get the information into the right hands, try to find out where she is if they took her. Can you imagine how scared that little girl is right now? And, frankly, the possibility that the traffickers might win pisses me off."

"Yeah, I know the feeling."

Leine leaned her head on the back of the couch and sighed. If she was completely honest with herself, the overriding reason was because she hoped that helping Mara would in some small way absolve her of having been a shitty mother to April all those years.

Hell, it was worth a try.

"Okay, Santa. I know you didn't invite me over here to make love. That much I understand. What's so important you'll risk your career consorting with a woman under investigation for murder?"

Jensen let go of her hand and shifted on the couch to face her. "There's new evidence against you. It shows you in L.A. on the dates of the murders."

Leine closed her eyes. "Let me guess. They have car rental agreements and airline manifests with my alias?"

"Yes."

"You do know how easy it is for Eric to create this 'evidence', right? That he can conjure the shit out of thin air?"

Jensen nodded. "I need the documents you sent to Eric's boss. I can get them to someone in the FBI who isn't beholden to the Agency. Go above Eric's boss' head."

Leine's smile held a sadness Jensen didn't like. "You're going to show those papers to the Vice President of the United States? Because, darling, that's who Eric's boss answers to."

Jensen leaned forward. "Didn't you say you thought Eric had intercepted the docs? That means there's a possibility his boss hasn't seen the information. My contact may be able to figure out some way to circumvent Eric's firewall, whatever it is, and get them into the right hands."

"I have no problem giving you the information. I just don't think it's going to work. Eric will figure out something to save his ass, he always does. There has to be a fall guy—and that's me." Leine rose to leave.

"It doesn't need to be that way, Leine." Jensen pulled her back down to the couch. "Stay," he whispered.

"I have to go." She looked away.

"Just for tonight."

"I—"

Jensen kissed away her objections.

They lay on his bed in the dark, his arms wrapped around her waist as he nuzzled her neck. Leine smiled at the tickling sensation. *Would it be such a bad thing to be able to stay here with Santa? Actually let herself be in love again?* She sighed at the thought. Her life was too complicated, too fraught with a past that wouldn't stay hidden, no matter what she tried. Santa had cracked open the wall she'd created around her emotions, giving her a glimpse of what her life could have been like had she chosen a different path.

There were so many barriers to a happy ending. Sure, if they succeeded in pinning the murders on Eric, then that would take care of one of the obstacles they faced together. But it would also create more problems than it solved.

Every time they came together, Leine could see her love for him reflected in his eyes. She knew that would never be enough. He'd always know what she'd done and that would affect their relationship. Loving a woman who had killed people for a living was not a good career move for a homicide detective. She'd hate herself if he had to give that up for her. Hell, she wasn't sure she could bring herself to trust another human being like she'd once trusted Carlos. And, last time she'd checked, trust was one of the main facets of a successful relationship.

There were other, more deadly concerns to take into consideration, as well.

"You're pretty quiet," Santa whispered in her ear. His warm breath skated across her skin. She settled deeper in his arms.

"Am I? This feels so good. I don't want to leave."

"Yeah. We fit, don't we?"

Leine turned to face him. "We need to talk."

"Uh-oh. Is this where you tell me it's been fun, but you need to move on?" The smile on his face faltered.

Leine ran her finger over his lips and along his jawline, trying to memorize his face. "You know this isn't going to work, right? That it's too dangerous?"

Santa closed his eyes and rolled onto his back; the absence of his warmth sent a shiver up her spine.

"No. I don't know that, Leine. What I know is I've never been in love, not before I met you." He opened his eyes and stared at the ceiling. "What I also know is you feel the same way about me, but for some reason you think it can't be. Is it so alien to you to be in love with a cop? Believe me, I've gone back and forth about your old job, and you know what my conclusion was? It's in the past and it doesn't matter."

"But your job—"

"I'm not gonna get canned for falling in love. Not unless you did those three cold cases and get popped, and I'm not willing to believe you're guilty. Now, maybe that's foolish and I'm looking at you through rose-colored glasses, but I think I'm more cool-headed than all that and can make a decision with my big head."

"Sounds like a speech you've had to deliver before. What does Putnam think?"

Santa shook his head. "It doesn't matter what he thinks. But for the record—" he sat up and slid against the headboard. "Putz has my back, no matter what. Always."

Leine moved over beside him. "They're making their play, darling. Let's say if, in a perfect world, Eric's boss gets the folder I'm going to give you. Let's also say that he crosschecks the information and believes it, then brings Eric up on charges. I might as well have a target tattooed onto my chest, because that's what I'll be, even if he doesn't go to ground and they wind up putting him in prison. And if I know Eric, and I do, you'll be in danger too, as well as my daughter. I can't let that happen. You both mean too much to me." She watched him, hoping he'd see the logic, but also hoping that he'd realize how much leaving him was going to cost her.

"I can take care of myself, Leine. And I can take care of you and April. Trust me."

"Let's not talk about this now." Leine ran her hand down his chest and along his stomach, then under the sheet bunched at his hips. He grabbed her arm, his gaze holding hers. A subtle shift occurred in the depths of his eyes before he pushed her back onto the mattress with her wrists above her head and covered her mouth with his.

Jensen woke to the morning traffic report blaring from his clock radio. Disoriented, he reached for Leine but found only sheets and a blanket. He looked over at the chair where she'd tossed her clothing and purse the night before. They were gone.

He pushed the sheet away and rose to get dressed as the reality of what happened the night before hit him. According to Leine, there could be no other choice. She'd send a courier to his house with the documents implicating Eric, but they wouldn't meet again. It was too dangerous.

Jensen dropped his jeans to the floor and sank onto the bed. He couldn't breathe. It felt like a battering ram had lodged itself in his solar plexus.

Leine was gone.

CHAPTER TWENTY-SEVEN

LEINE LOGGED INTO EMAIL ON her tablet, clicked open the message from DNAsty Labs and scanned the test results. Jean wasn't a match. She hit print and pulled the hard copy off the printer on the desk. Then she logged out and powered off the computer.

She stood and walked over to her bed. A spacious leather bag lay on the floor. She bent over and tapped the wall near the headboard with the side of her fist. A spring-loaded door opened to reveal a mini Uzi—an Israeli-made submachine gun—and several other weapons secreted inside the wall. Once she had everything in the bag, she closed the door and returned to the living room.

She'd paid cash up front for several months' rent, and the manager of the apartment complex hadn't asked for personal details like her name or occupation. The little bungalow she'd originally rented when she first came to L.A. had been a good size and location, but the memories were too fresh, so she'd found the apartment.

The place was average in size and unremarkable, with two bedrooms in case April wanted to spend the night. No art hung on the walls, no mail littered the countertops. There was nothing unusual in the apartment that might be traced back to Leine save for the tablet, and she kept that with her. Not even the dishes in the cupboard; all nondescript, white dinnerware from Ikea.

Old habits died hard.

Once she made sure the windows and slider were secure, she turned off the lights and walked out the door, locking it behind her. Then she took the stairs to the sublevel garage and got in her non-descript tan, four-door sedan. She wouldn't be coming back. If the files made it to Eric's boss, it wouldn't be long before Eric came after her. She wouldn't be safe.

As she drove to the Krav Maga studio in west Los Angeles, she ran through possible scenarios involving the DNA test results in her mind. The first, best possibility involved Miles reading the email and realizing if Jean had lied about her being his sister, then she might also be lying about everything else. Miles would then banish her from his life and take out a restraining order against her.

The next best possibility involved him confronting Jean and her coming up with a good explanation. The report from DNAsty Labs left no doubt in Leine's mind she was conning him. Why, or for what, Leine wasn't sure, but she sure as hell wasn't going to let her take advantage of Miles' trusting nature. Let her come up with a solid reason, Leine mused. She'd be interested to hear it.

That left the question of Mara. Was she really her mother? Leine had become even more vested in finding her, knowing Jean lied. Now that she was between jobs, she had more free time to devote to locating her. Jensen had assured her he'd make sure they flagged the report from Bauer.

Leine inhaled sharply. The thought of never seeing him again tore at her with such force it stole her breath. She shoved the feelings deep and tried to focus on Mara. The more people they had out looking for her, the better. Jean's subterfuge voided any consideration Leine may have had regarding her decision to keep things quiet. Besides, she was no longer on Miles' payroll and felt no loyalty toward the woman.

She pulled to the curb in front of the studio and parked. Tucking the email into her purse, she walked through the large glass doors and down the hall to where Miles and Rico were practicing. April had wanted to join, but Leine told her she'd teach her more in-depth techniques herself and she'd agreed. She still wasn't excited about the burgeoning romance between Miles and her daughter and didn't want her anywhere near Rico Pallini.

Leine stood in the doorway and watched Miles and Rico spar as the instructor coached them. What Miles possessed in athleticism and agility, Rico more than made up for in determination and strength. Leine's initial decision to refer them to another venue had been astute, especially in light of her being canned. A blond man with a crew-cut dressed in black with a well-defined physique leaned against a nearby wall with his arms crossed. He straightened when he saw Leine. *Must be the new bodyguard.*

Rico caught sight of her first.

"What're you stopping for?" Miles asked. Rico cocked his head at Leine. Miles turned and lifted his chin in acknowledgement. "Leine."

"Did Mara show up last night?" Leine asked.

"No. But we're going again tonight." His eyebrows came together in a frown. "What do you want? We're busy."

"I'm only here to deliver the DNA results." Leine unfolded the paper with the email and held it out to him. "Jean's not your sister."

Miles shook his head. "Don't care." He turned back to his instructor and nodded for him to continue.

"What do you mean, you don't care? Jean's been lying to you all along. Miles. She's using you. I'm not sure why, but whatever the reason, this changes things."

Miles stopped sparring with the instructor and walked over to where Leine stood. He grabbed a bottle of water off the table next to her and took a drink, then wiped the sweat off his forehead with a towel that was sitting next to the water.

"It doesn't matter. Don't you get it? I don't care that she's not my sister. I've gotten to know her and I care about her. She lied. So what? She's got her reasons. Haven't you ever lied?" He dropped the towel on the table. "She's lost her little girl and she's desperate. If I thought lying about whether I was related to someone would help me find my daughter, I'd damn well do it, too."

"What if she's not Mara's mother?"

Miles shook his head. "I don't buy it. She's too concerned. She's never not been concerned the entire time she's lived in my house. If she was helping the men who were trying to kidnap me, like you initially thought, they'd have already done it—there were plenty of times someone could have grabbed me. She knew my schedule, had the floor plan of my house. That's because the only thing she's interested in is getting her daughter back. It's been her overriding concern from day one."

"Leave him alone, Leine," Rico added, coming to stand next to Miles. "He's right. No matter how you play it, she's scared for her daughter and wants to get her back. If Miles can help her do that, he will." He looked at her with what appeared to be disdain. "You don't work for him anymore. Let it go. This won't get your job back." Rico's tone dripped with scorn, as though having a job working for Miles was something Leine cared about. She almost laughed.

"I don't want my job back, Rico. I only care what's best for Mara." She turned to Miles. "It's your call. I'm just the messenger." She leaned forward and slid the folded email into the chest pocket of his t-shirt. "You need to think long and hard about this, Miles." Then she turned and walked out the door.

Santiago Jensen entered the dimly lit bar and took a seat facing the door. He laid the manila envelope on the table and ordered a club soda with lime from the bartender. It was early in the day and there were few customers and no other wait staff.

The envelope contained a copy of the damning information Leine had attempted to send to Eric's boss. Jensen had read the documents and been floored by the implications. There were transcripts of calls to illegal arms dealers, extreme Islamic regimes, a notorious African warlord, and the leader of a ruthless Mexican drug cartel with whom Eric had non-Agency sanctioned dealings. In addition, the information included detailed reports of contract hits he ordered using Agency personnel and resources that were purportedly kept off the books. Whoever possessed the information would be in grave danger.

Jensen sipped his club soda and stared at the envelope. If everything in it could be verified, then not only was Leine telling the truth about her old boss, but she was in deeper than he had realized.

Sunlight streamed into the bar as the front door opened, illuminating the stained carpeting and well-worn tables and chairs. His FBI contact, Daniel Babcock, spotted him and walked over to the table.

"Danny. Good to see you." Jensen extended his hand.

"Always a pleasure to meet with L.A.'s finest. How you been, Santa?" Daniel shook his hand, a smile on his face. The chair scraped across the floor as he pulled it out and sat down on the other side of the table. "To what do I owe this occasion? You were pretty vague in your message."

Jensen slid the envelope toward him. "It's all inside. There's information regarding a high-ranking official in a shadow organization used by the United States referred to simply as the Agency." Daniel's expression remained neutral but Jensen sensed him stiffen. He continued. "There's currently an investigation underway in my department of three unsolved murders. I believe if this information is given to the appropriate party, the suspect they're investigating will be exonerated and the real shooter be brought to justice."

"Why come to me? Why not go to your CO?"

The bartender appeared and asked Daniel if he'd like anything. He shook his head no and the bartender went back to polishing glasses. Jensen waited until he was out of earshot before continuing.

"Because the same information was sent once before and the individual identified in the documents allegedly intercepted the copies. We believe he's manipulating evidence to pin the murders on an innocent fall-guy."

Calling Leine innocent may have ordinarily been a stretch, but in Jensen's line of work, as well as the FBI's, lines drawn between the innocent and the guilty were frequently faint.

"That's a pretty serious charge. Are you absolutely sure?"

"Yes."

Daniel pulled the contents out of the envelope and scanned them. After a few moments, he returned the papers and leaned back in his chair, a wary expression on his face. "Santa, if I'm going to do what I think you're asking me to do, then I'll need more than your assurance this information is accurate."

"Tell me what you want and I'll get it."

Leine pressed the end button on her phone as she sat in the coffee shop, a double espresso and an untouched Rice Krispy bar on the table in front of her.

The person she'd just spoken to was a last resort contact from her old life, and it turned out to be a dead end. No one had useful information for finding Mara. They assured her they would keep her in their databases and contact Leine if something came up. Trafficking organizations were a dime a dozen, she was told, and it was next to impossible to track them. Leine had one of her friends run the black BMW's license plate, but it was registered to a shell corporation and the security surrounding it was labyrinthine. It would take too long to unravel the convoluted paper trail to find the original owner. Mara would be long gone, or dead.

Leine took a drink of her coffee, considering her next move. There was one last option, but she wanted to exhaust all resources before she pursued that avenue. The theme from the Godfather broke through her thoughts and she answered her phone on the second ring.

"Leine? Lou Stokes here."

Leine's heart rate picked up. "Hi Lou. What's going on?"

"I found out some more information on that twelve-year-old runaway."

"Great. What have you got?"

"Not so great. Word on the street is she was bought by some rich dirt bag here in town who likes fresh talent for his own private cinematic experience. He's putting massive pressure on whoever sold her to him to find her."

"Any names?"

Lou sighed. "None. The guy's identity is well protected. The only reason I received this much info is because some thug, probably one of the trafficker's minions, let it slip to a source after a night of carousing."

"That's more than we had before. Do you by any chance have the thug's name?"

"Yuri something. Sorry I can't be of more help."

"That's more help than you know, Lou."

CHAPTER TWENTY-EIGHT

NADJA IMPORTS LOOKED LESS SINISTER in daylight. The West Hollywood import store was buzzing with customers and deliveries as Leine pulled into the parking lot across the street. The last time she visited had been late at night and she'd barely escaped with her life. The feel of the nine millimeter under her shirt reassured her. The Russians would be more circumspect in daylight.

Too many witnesses.

Leine crossed the busy street and entered through the glass double doors. Inside, the front section was stuffed floor-to-ceiling with Russian icons, gold-leafed crèches, hand-carved furniture, nesting dolls, and lacquer boxes, as well as other merchandise from the Eastern Bloc. A fine layer of dust had settled on most of the items, suggesting walk-in buyers weren't the owner's main consideration. Leine assumed the illegal arms and drugs they distributed were hidden in the back warehouse.

A compact, dark-haired man materialized from the back, wiping his hands on a towel. The smile on his ruddy face disappeared and his step faltered when he caught sight of his visitor. After a beat, another smile spread across his face. She had to hand it to him, he recovered quickly.

"What have we here? An honored guest has come to visit." He stretched his arms wide, palms open. "To what do I owe this immense pleasure?" The coldness in his brown eyes belied the friendly tone. Leine remembered he had the same look when he pointed a gun at her on her last visit.

She raised her hands, careful to keep them within range of her gun. "I come in peace, Vladimir. I need information, that's all."

Vladimir chuckled and shook his head. "And why do you think I would give to you that information, assuming I have what you want? If I remember correctly, the last time you were here, you took valuable item from me."

"True, but my daughter was in danger. I did what I had to." Leine watched him closely as she lowered her arms. She wasn't here to fight. She had no advantage other than the gun in her shoulder holster, and that would vaporize as soon as the first shot was fired. Leine counted at least a half-dozen of his people near the back loading bays, and that didn't include the rest of the neighborhood.

The bell on the door tinkled as a hipster couple entered the store. Leine turned back to Vladimir. "Is there somewhere more private?"

Valdimir nodded and swept his hand toward the back. Leine walked past him and headed to the office. "Someone will be right with you," he said to the couple, and followed Leine.

Leine had a seat on one of two white leather chairs across from Vladimir. He scowled and opened the top drawer of his desk. Leine tensed and moved for her gun, but instead of a weapon he pulled out a half-empty bottle of vodka and two ornate shot glasses. She relaxed and rested her hand on the arm of the chair.

"Join me," he said, and poured two shots. Leine accepted one and threw it back. The liquid warmed her throat. She set the glass on the desk. He did the same and wiped his mouth with the back of his hand. "You know, after you killed Borys and stole gun of the Frenchman, I vowed vengeance. Now you walk into my store, showing no fear, asking for favor." He moved her shot glass alongside his and poured two more drinks. Then he slid one toward her and drank the other before continuing.

"The only reason your brains are not spilled out on my floor is you did world a favor by killing the Frenchman. But, you also killed one of my men. I think this makes us even. I give you gun, no strings attached," he said with a shrug. "It was piece of shit anyway."

"So this means I owe you a favor if you have the information I'm searching for," Leine replied.

Vladimir nodded. "Exactly. Your services will come in handy."

"I'm not in that life anymore, Vlad."

"You are if we continue conversation."

"I will do many things, but I no longer kill for money or favor. We will have to come up with something we can both agree upon."

Vladimir appeared to consider her statement. Then he nodded his head. "You still have valuable contacts, yes? This I will use in future. Agreed?"

"Agreed." Leine didn't want to consent to anything, but sometimes you needed to do things you didn't like. Finding Mara was one of those times. She continued. "I'm looking for a twelve-year-old American girl with unusual green eyes. Currently she is missing and believed to be hiding out on the streets of L.A. Information I've received suggests that perhaps she had originally been taken by a group originating in Moscow who are also looking for her. I need to find her first." Leine left out that Mara may already be in the hands of the traffickers. She was curious to see how Vladimir reacted.

He watched her through hooded eyes as he listened. When she finished, he remained silent for a moment. He cleared his throat and squinted at her as he poured a third shot and drank it. He offered another to Leine, but she declined.

"This girl, what is her name?"

"Mara."

"I may have what you need." He leaned forward and rested his elbows on the desk. "You can be sure this is not work of Russian organization. The number one reason being they don't deal with American children, only young women of consenting age from what you call Eastern bloc. Is still USSR to me." He waved away the implication that the USSR was no longer in its former glory. "They're happy to become part of organization. What would they have if they stayed? Poverty, disease and death. This way, they receive food and place to live."

Leine wasn't about to argue the finer points of conscripting young women into sex trafficking with Vladimir. To him, it was a money-making venture, pure and simple.

"And, you say this girl escaped?" Vladimir shook his head, his laugh scornful. "Reason number two: she would not have escaped."

"Can you tell me who wants to find her?"

"His name is Greg Kirchner. He was small-time hustler who made name for himself securing children for rich old men." Vladimir spat the words as though they left a bad taste in his mouth. "He operates out of office in Encino. There is no honor in this. In my organization, having sex with children is punishable by death. They are exterminated like the rat-fucks they are."

He seemed to know a lot about the non-Russian trafficker. Leine pressed on. "I was told a man with a Russian accent was one of the men who had taken her. Any idea who that might be?"

Vladimir rubbed his eyes with the palms of his hands and sighed. "There is much pain in my heart to say this terrible thing." He frowned as he fingered the label on the vodka bottle. "My nephew on my wife's side, Yuri, is one you speak of, although he's from Ukraine. It was his cousin you killed last time you were here. If you think he will help you, you are mistaken."

The name matched the one Lou gave her. Vladimir hadn't lied to save family. She wondered why. "Where can I find him?"

Vladimir glanced at the ceiling before answering. "He sometimes drinks at Baba Ganesh. You must promise me you will not kill him. My wife would never let me hear end of it."

"How good is he?"

Vladimir shook his head and powered back another shot. He rested the glass on the table and looked her steadily in the eyes. "He is disgrace to our family. I think you will have to convince him to help you." He smiled. "I doubt you will have problem with that, yes?"

"Yes." Leine rose to leave. "Thank you, Vladimir."

Vladimir bowed his head. "You are welcome. One of my people will contact you in future for favor. Please, do not kill."

"As long as it's by phone or letter, you can rest assured I will not."

CHAPTER TWENTY-NINE

ABA GANESH SMELLED LIKE SPILLED booze and sweat. Two dancers in varying stages of undress wearing veils edged in silver and gold coins gyrated to a Middle Eastern techno beat. The rectangular stage, situated in the middle of the club, was surrounded by a chrome and Lucite bar with LED lights embedded in the handrail. A lone bartender was busy working a small crowd of Asian men, obviously drunk, who whistled and waved twenty dollar bills at the dancers.

Leine scanned the club, looking for someone fitting Vladimir's description of Yuri. A thin man with a crooked nose and bruises under his eyes sat by himself at the end of the bar. Shoulders slumped forward, he stared at one of the dancers, a partially consumed drink in front of him. Leine recognized him as one of the men who was chasing Mara at Grauman's Theater during Miles' handprint ceremony. Keeping her eye on the bouncer standing sentry at the far end of the room, she slowed her pace, circled the bar and slipped up behind him, gun drawn.

"Just the man I'm looking for," she said into his ear as she removed his gun from his waistband and slid it into the back of her pants, under her jacket. Yuri jumped but stilled as soon as he became aware of her semiautomatic pushed into his side. He turned his head, his eyes widening when he saw who held the gun.

"You—" he sputtered, his face growing dark. "I should rip out your throat with my bare hands for what you did to Borys." His breathing came in short bursts. Leine had to turn her face away from the stench of booze and bad gums. A strange whistling sound emanated from his nose. He closed his eyes and took a deep breath. Leine shoved the gun harder into his side.

"You might want to consider why I'm here," she said.

A bead of sweat formed on his forehead and tracked its way down his face. His Adam's apple bobbed as he tried to swallow. "I don't know what you are saying. How did you find me?"

"The how isn't important. The why is." Leine scanned the bar again to make sure no one was close enough to see the gun or notice Yuri's discomfiture. "I need you to tell me where the girl is."

Yuri stiffened. "I don't know what you are talking about."

"Oh, I think you do, Yuri. And if you don't tell me, I will break more than your nose."

"Stand in line," Yuri replied. The bravado in his voice held a slight tremor. He lifted the drink to his lips and threw it back, then banged it on the bar. The bartender didn't bat an eyelash, preferring the large group of paying customers at the other end. "I will be dead soon."

"Then you shouldn't have a problem telling me where Greg Kirchner is."

Yuri looked at Leine, a smirk on his face. "You are crazy if you think I would tell you this."

"Take a walk with me, Yuri. Now." Leine grabbed hold of his arm and wrenched it back and up, forcing his hand between his shoulder blades until Yuri yelped in pain. She felt around his back and under his arms looking for additional weapons. When she didn't find any, she dragged him off the barstool.

"I haven't paid—"

"I've got it," Leine said as she threw some bills near his empty glass and pushed him through the bar to the back door. When they hit daylight, she kicked the metal door shut and released his arm.

Yuri turned to face her, rubbing his shoulder. "What the fuck do you think I'm going to tell you? I'm not going to give you directions where you can find my boss. You will just have to 'Goggle' it."

"That's Google, idiot, and yes, you will give me directions because if you don't I will take you somewhere quiet and perform painful acts, not only on your face but other places as well." Leine indicated his crotch with the barrel of her gun. "By your reaction, you know who I am, right? Did you hear how they found the Frenchman, what kind of condition he was in?" Leine hadn't tortured the Frenchman before firing the shot that killed him, but Yuri didn't have to know that. His uncertain expression gave Leine the response she was looking for.

"Well?" she asked.

Yuri bowed his head and crossed his arms. Leine sighed and pulled back the gun's slide and aimed it at his head. He dropped his hands and stood at attention.

"Walk to the tan car over there."

"They don't have the girl. If they did, I would not be alive."

At that moment, a black BMW careened around the corner, tires spitting rocks, passenger side window lowered to reveal a man's arm holding a small submachine gun.

"Down!" Leine grabbed Yuri by the shirt collar and threw him to the ground behind an SUV. She dropped and rolled behind him and came up firing. The bullets from the other gun strafed the dirt next to her, kicking up pebbles and dust. She tracked the car as it drove past her and fired at the open window. One of the bullets hit the man's arm and the gun dropped to the ground. The BMW swerved and skidded to a stop in a cloud of dust.

Leine dragged Yuri up off the gravel and shoved him toward a cement barrier as she took cover behind a red Buick before the driver exited the car. Her heart racing, she reached into the cargo pocket of her pants for more ammo and replaced the spent magazine from her gun. Then she took a deep breath and stood.

The driver's shadow indicated he had crouched behind the front wheel well of the BMW. He popped up near the front corner panel and peppered the Buick with bullets. Leine returned fire. Her shots ricocheted off the hood next to him. He ducked, then came back up, fired a couple of shots and ducked again. Pieces of the Buick's side mirror glanced off her arm. The back window exploded from the inside the BMW as the man she'd wounded shot through the glass. He wasn't as good with his left hand, and the bullets went wide. Leine took aim and fired through the opening, hitting him in the left shoulder. His head disappeared as he fell back.

The driver reappeared, but Leine was ready for him. The bullet carved through the center of his forehead and exploded out the back. He snapped backward and disappeared behind the car.

Leine turned in time to see Yuri running toward the street. She sprinted after him, catching him before he made it out of the parking lot.

He bent over, hands on his knees and tried to catch his breath. Leine glanced at his feet while she paced off the adrenaline.

"Those aren't the shoes to wear when you need to run, Yuri,"

He stared at his square-toed dress shoes and shrugged. "Yeah, but they look good."

The sound of sirens in the distance told Leine it was time to leave. She grabbed hold of his shirt collar and pulled him toward her car. "You're coming with me."

They headed west through Beverly Hills toward the 405 freeway. Yuri still refused to tell her where in Encino his boss' office was located, but Leine had confidence she'd be able to persuade him. He stared out the window at the palm tree-lined streets with a glum look.

"You know, when I came to US I thought everybody got to live in one of those." He pointed to a brick and stucco mansion as they passed, set back from an imposing iron gate with at least two luxury cars in view. He sighed and leaned his head back. "And now I am dead. I will never bring my mother to Los Angeles to see Hollywood Boulevard or be able to take her on the Map of Stars."

"Yeah, L.A. can be a bitch, can't she?"

Yuri's laugh sounded more like an aborted hiccup. He wiped at his eyes. "You aren't kidding."

They drove in silence until they reached Encino. Leine exited and pulled into a vacant lot behind an empty insurance building, well hidden from the main road. She turned to Yuri. Perspiration rolled down the sides of his face. "Time to tell me where I'm going."

He shook his head, his eyes pleading. "No."

"Look, Yuri. I saved your life back at Baba Ganesh, agreed?"

He nodded.

"Then I say you owe me. If you don't tell me what I want to know, I will first try to make you see it my way." She indicated the vacant lot with a meaningful stare. "If that doesn't work, and I'm pretty sure it will, I will deliver you back to the bar. I don't think the people who are trying to kill you will be very happy about what happened back there. At least one man is dead and the other is going to be out of commission for a very long time."

Yuri didn't say anything for a long moment. Then he sat straighter in his seat, apparently having made up his mind. "You are right. I owe you my life. You're looking for the girl. I can't tell you where my boss is. For this, he would torture me before he killed me, but I can tell you she tried to contact Miles Fournier, the actor."

"That's it? That's all you've got?" Leine pointed her gun at him. "Sorry buddy, but you're going to have to come up with something a lot better than that."

"No—wait. She was seen at restaurant he frequents. The Briar Cliff. I know this because I myself located the information."

"You mean from that guy you put in the hospital?"

Yuri's mouth opened and closed like a fish stranded on gravel. "I…how…"

"I've already spoken with him. He's going to be okay, in case you were interested. Although he will need a lot of physical therapy to be able to walk again."

He eyed the gun with unease. "You must let me explain—"

Leine frowned and shook her head. "No, Yuri. It's quite clear what you were doing." She leaned closer. "It's kind of like what's happening now, except I'm not going to go as easy on you if you don't give me the information I need."

Yuri swallowed and licked his lips. His hand trembled as he wiped his forehead. She could tell by the look on his face he was searching for something to say, anything to make this crazy woman put the gun down.

Exactly what she wanted.

"All I know is she hasn't been back to restaurant. The police somehow found out about her; an unmarked car has been parked there every night." His voice wavered. "They were trying to kill me at Baba Ganesh. Why tell me important information when I am going to be dead?"

"Good point. Then it's even more vital that you tell me how to find Greg."

His breath caught and he let out a half-sob. "You don't understand. There's no way you can get inside the building. He will only allow people he knows through the door."

"Well, he knows you, right?"

His face drained to a pasty shade.

Leine patted his arm. "It's settled, then. You'll help me get in to see Greg and I'll let you go. Deal?"

Yuri closed his eyes and leaned his head back. "Deal," he whispered.

She slid her gun into her shoulder holster and put the car in gear. Then she pulled out of the parking lot, driving slowly through the neighborhood, the latest recession evident from the dark interior of the empty buildings.

The force of the impact from the other vehicle threw them both forward into the dash. Dazed, Leine shook her head to clear it. She stomped on the accelerator, but the SUV stayed with them. Leine made a hard right around the next corner. The other vehicle dropped back slightly before it surged forward and smashed into the sedan's rear corner, causing the car to fishtail. She steered out of the slide and turned again. The SUV drove up beside the sedan and broadsided them, sending them over the curb and into a parking lot. The truck followed and slammed into the back end, shoving the car over a raised median, high-centering them.

The car lurched to a stop. Leine unbuckled her seatbelt and dropped down in her seat, pulling her gun from its holster. Yuri followed her lead, the whites of his eyes visible. "Shit—" Yuri started to say, but Leine held her finger to her lips.

She reached up to position the rearview mirror to get a look at the hulking SUV now affixed to the trunk of her car. No one occupied the driver's seat. No gunfire erupted from the other vehicle, which was odd. Leine glanced at Yuri, the bruises under his eyes more pronounced because of the ashen pallor of his face.

"Stay down," she said in a low voice. Yuri didn't argue and slid the rest of the way onto the floor. Leine wasn't about to let the driver of the SUV gun down Yuri. He still had too much information she needed.

She eased her door open and crouched low as she stepped outside. Alert for movement, she crept around the car, edging closer to the truck and stopping to listen at varying intervals. The silence struck her as odd. Typically, when someone made that kind of grand entrance they used the surprise generated to complete their objective. In this case, Yuri was still alive and so was she.

She continued around the vehicle, checking underneath the SUV for a visual, but saw nothing. The driver could be standing behind a wheel, or might still be inside. She eased her way toward the rear of the truck, scanning the area to make sure someone hadn't slipped around from behind to take Yuri out.

With her back to the SUV and gun in front of her, Leine rounded the end of the vehicle. The kick came out of nowhere and temporarily paralyzed her right hand. Her gun fell from her grasp and clattered to the ground. The next one hit her in the ribs. She staggered backward and turned as a wall of t-shirt-wearing muscle crashed into her and they fell to the ground, knocking the wind out of her. Ignoring the stabbing pain in her side, Leine brought her knee up and at the same time grabbed the barrel of the man's gun, barely forcing it away as he pulled the trigger.

The report was deafening.

Her ears rang, the muffled sound like that of sand particles shifting underwater. His other hand closed around her throat in an attempt to crush her windpipe. Focused only on survival, Leine gripped the gun barrel with her left hand and tried to pry his fingers off her neck with the numb one. She managed to bend his hand far enough the wrong way to put pressure on his trigger finger and loosen his hold on the gun. In response, he let go of her neck and moved away to retain the grip, creating space between them. Recognizing her razor-thin advantage, she wrenched the gun from his grasp and thrust her knee into his groin. She was rewarded with a sharp intake of breath.

His face a grimace, the man grabbed her neck with both hands and squeezed. She pushed hard against him with her left hand and knee, creating enough room to maneuver the gun between them. Dark spots appeared in her periphery and her eyesight dimmed as oxygen deprivation threatened to overtake her. Summoning a last surge of strength, she willed her right hand to respond, rammed the forty-five into his solar plexus, and pulled the trigger.

Eyes wide, his mouth open in an 'o', he gripped his stomach where the bullet entered his abdomen. A dark red stain appeared and spread across his shirt. He glanced at his hand, now covered in blood, and then at Leine. It was the first time she'd gotten a good look at him. She'd seen him somewhere before.

Leine shoved him backward and he crumpled onto his side. Coughing, she winced as she struggled to her feet. She tried to take a breath and doubled over from the searing-hot pain that arced across her ribcage. She took a moment to recover, then staggered to the SUV, hand gripping her side. After reassuring herself that no one else waited for her inside the truck, she returned to search the man's clothes for identification.

His pockets were empty. Leine wasn't surprised. Memories swam their way to the surface as she studied his face. It didn't take long before she realized how she knew him. Startled, she stepped away from the body, the implication clear. She shook it off and opened the passenger door to search the interior of the truck.

On the console was a manila folder marked *Confidential* with her picture clipped to the front. She skimmed its contents then closed the folder and tucked it under her arm as she searched the rest of the vehicle, ice-cold awareness creeping up her spine.

Finding nothing else of value except the keys in the ignition, Leine exited the truck to assess the damage to her car. The rear end was severely impacted, but if she could uncouple it from the SUV and push it off the median, it would be drivable. As she skirted the side of the car she realized Yuri was no longer hiding on the floor. In fact, he was no longer in the car. She scanned the street in both directions, but there was no sign of him. Her struggle with the assailant had been the perfect distraction for his escape.

She climbed into the SUV and gingerly leaned against the seat as she started the engine and shifted into low gear. The sound of metal against metal set Leine's teeth on edge. An agony in time passed as she braced herself and tried to find a comfortable position while she pushed her car off the curb. As soon as all four wheels hit asphalt, and the SUV disengaged from the back bumper, she returned to her car. She pulled out of the lot and turned right onto the busy boulevard. The new evidence chilled her as the realization spread.

The left side of the folder bore a familiar stamp.

The Agency.

CHAPTER THIRTY

GREG KIRCHNER GLANCED AT THE columns of numbers in front of him, not registering the massive profit listed at the bottom of the spreadsheet. He'd just received a phone call informing him of a skirmish at Baba Ganesh, where two of his best shooters had been gunned down. Yuri, the little weasel, had escaped. Greg had no idea how the stupid shit made it out alive, but word was he'd had help.

He'd made sure Ned wasn't having a drink with Yuri when he sent in his team. Ned proved to be worth much more in the brains department than Yuri could ever dream of being. Greg decided he'd given Yuri enough time to find the girl. With his discovery of Ned's value, he felt justified eliminating the idiot Ukrainian from the payroll.

And now he was on the run. Greg slammed his hand on the desk, making the stapler dance. His client was putting pressure on him to find the girl and tie up loose ends. Yuri was one of those loose ends, but now he couldn't even point to that little victory. At least the other play they'd put into place to find Mara was active, although they'd hit a snag there, too.

Greg rose from his chair and tossed the spreadsheet on the desk. Moving to the window, he gazed at the park below his office. If they didn't find Mara and deliver her to the client within the next twenty-four hours, he was finished. There was no way his reputation would recover from *losing the fucking product*. The client, Stone Ellison, had too much reach. In this business, word of mouth was everything.

Greg pivoted at the knock on the door. One of his employees, a barrel-chested man with a shaved head and muscular arms covered in tattoos stood in the doorway.

"What the fuck do you want?" Greg muttered as he proceeded to straighten the papers on his desk.

"We got some good news."

Greg glanced up from the stack of spreadsheets and squinted. "Yeah?"

"Basso's history."

"She's gone? Why? I thought Fournier was smitten."

"Nope. She's number one on his shit list. Apparently, not only does Fournier think she scared the kid off at the restaurant, but she pulled a piece on Selena in the can and she played it like Basso was threatening to shoot her."

"Good to know." An interesting development. Selena had turned out to be surprisingly good at subterfuge. Greg smiled to himself. It had been a stroke of genius enlisting her help. The information he'd gotten from Fournier's agent made it easy to get the actor to believe her story about being his long-lost sister. He'd gambled that DNA testing would take longer than the amount of time he needed to get Mara back, and so far, he'd been right. He was running out of options, though. That's what made Saturday so important.

Greg was going to have to tweak the plan. The recent turn of events wasn't going to help with the new security contingent around Miles. On the other hand, he wouldn't have to worry about that LAPD dick, Santiago Jensen, showing up. He needed to make a phone call. Greg picked up his phone and looked pointedly at his employee.

"You mind?"

The man blinked a couple of times and stepped into the hall.

"Wait a minute." Greg covered the phone with his hand. "You got the layout for Saturday?"

"Yeah. What do you need?"

"I need you to take care of Selena once we get the girl."

The guy nodded and started to leave.

"One other thing. You know Yuri?"

"Yeah."

"Do the same for him."

Leine checked her watch and logged onto her computer. She ignored the high pitched screech as the barista foamed milk in a stainless container at the front of the café, and typed in the password for her email.

She'd taken to using the Wi-Fi at populated venues, and never used the same place twice. Even though she knew it wasn't fail-safe, it was better than establishing a routine and inviting her execution.

She scanned the subject line of her emails and opened the one that read "Your Inquiry" from a firm she'd used in the past to check into a target's history. She'd given them a glass she'd taken from Jean's room with a clear set of fingerprints. The investigators had encountered a problem with the information Leine had provided. She skimmed the rest of the message and double-clicked one of two attachments. A full arrest record appeared on the screen, but the name didn't match and the address wasn't in Nevada.

There must be some mistake. Leine scanned the report. A DUI from that past May was listed as well as several other alcohol-related misdemeanors spanning the last ten years. Everything dovetailed with what the first security check revealed, as well as what Jean had told them.

Leine clicked on the other attachment, a .jpeg. The file opened and she stared at the photograph.

The mug shot showed Jean, but the name below the picture was the same as that on the arrest record: Selena Fullerton. Leine returned to the email from the investigative firm and read it more closely.

As soon as she was finished, she hit *forward* and typed in Miles' email address. This was incontrovertible proof that Jean/Selena had deceived him about everything from being related to being Mara's mother. Miles had to take action now. Leine added a note explaining the photograph's origins and hit *send*. She wasn't sure he'd open the email from her, much less an attachment. There had to be a way to get the picture to him before Jean/Selena did whatever it was she was determined to do.

Leine had argued with herself whether she should even try to change Miles' mind, and came up with the same answer repeatedly. She'd actually grown to like the guy, as frustrating as he was to deal with on a professional basis, and hated to see him being used for whatever purpose Selena had in mind. She also felt a deep connection to Mara and couldn't stand the thought of a young girl on the brink of adulthood, being thrust into a bleak life of misery and pain, only to be thrown away at some later date.

If Selena was actually working for the kidnappers, why hadn't they made their move already? Was it because Leine had been working for Miles? Were they waiting for her to leave? There'd been a couple of instances where she was off duty, but they were few and far between. Still, Selena could have contacted the kidnappers and told them Leine was out for the afternoon or evening. Leine hadn't exactly told them when she was going to be back, so that may have stopped their move.

But the theory wasn't logical. No one knew her background. To Selena and Miles, Leine was simply a security specialist, not an ex-assassin. Why would they wait until she was gone? Miles had immediately hired someone to take her place. Leine pushed the idea to the back of her mind. There had to be something else, some other reason for her lies.

Leine put her tablet into her purse and finished her cappuccino. She needed to talk to Miles, even if it meant physically putting the photo of Selena in his hand. She checked the date on her watch. Friday the sixteenth. Miles' premiere was the next day. She'd arrive early, take a chance he'd speak with her. At the same time, Leine would be there in case Mara tried to get to Miles again. This would be the girl's last chance to connect with the star; afterward, he was leaving on a three-week trip to promote the movie overseas.

Leine rose to leave and was walking out the door when it hit her. She hesitated, moving only when one of the café's customers walked around her in order to exit. Why hadn't she seen it before? Of course Selena was trying to get to Mara, but not because she was her mother.

She was working for the traffickers.

CHAPTER THIRTY-ONE

MILES TOOK ONE LAST LOOK at himself in the mirror and adjusted his jacket. T-minus two hours before the big premiere. Jean stood behind him and smiled at his reflection.

"You look fantastic, Miles."

"Thanks."

Jean tilted her head to the side. "What's wrong? You seem distant."

"Thinking about the premiere, is all."

"And that we might finally find Mara? Oh, Miles," she said, beaming. "Soon I'll be able to hold my baby in my arms again."

Miles stared at her reflection, fighting the words he wanted to say. This wasn't the time or the place. He'd tried to ignore the results from the DNA test, but Leine's insistence that Jean was up to something more had wormed its way into his mind and settled like a chancre, eating away at the happiness he'd found knowing he had a family. He turned from the mirror and went to the kitchen where he opened the freezer and grabbed a pre-made container of tequila slushy.

173

"Shit." He slammed the plastic bottle on the counter. The drink had frozen solid—he hadn't used enough tequila. He placed it in the microwave, hit thirty seconds and leaned against the counter to wait. He hated that Leine planted doubt about Jean in his mind. Now he scrutinized everything she did, searching for the lie in her statements. He'd quietly notified his security staff to watch her. They probably thought he was paranoid, but he didn't care. What was he going to do? Was Mara even her daughter? Why would Jean lie about getting her back?

Jean came up beside him and placed her hand on his arm. Miles jerked away and spun to face her, his anger roiling to the surface. Her eyes widened and she shrank back.

"Dammit, Jean. Why'd you lie to me?"

Jean looked as though he'd slapped her. "What do you mean? I never—"

Miles raised his hand. "Stop, Jean. Just stop. Everything you say sounds like a lie. Look," he paused, fighting for control. "Before Leine left, she ran your DNA to verify you were who you said you were, but the results came back negative." He crossed his arms. "There's no way in hell you're my sister."

Jean's face drained of color with the exception of her cheeks, which were two bright pink spots. "That's a lie." Her voice rose, matching the color in her face. "How dare you run a test without my permission?" She clasped her shaking hands together. "Where did you get the sample? How do you know it wasn't contaminated? Don't you have to have a swab or something?"

"It was hair from your brush."

"No." She appeared to deflate before him. "That can't be. I...I'm...my mother told me—" she stammered.

Miles' anger began to recede, replaced by a sorrow so deep, so cutting, he was sure he'd crack open and his insides would spill out. The sensation was new—he hadn't allowed himself to feel real emotion since his parents were killed. He became skilled at pretending by studying other people's responses to his actions, all the while keeping a part of himself locked away and unreachable. It's what made him a good actor. At least he thought so, until now.

Now, that part of him dropped like a curtain on the final night of a long-running show. Stripped bare, he realized he was experiencing raw, visceral emotion for the first time since the accident. He squeezed his eyes closed and tried to stop the wave of despair threatening to overwhelm him. Taking a few deep breaths he opened his eyes. Jean watched him closely, a look of alarm on her face.

"Please, let me explain." Jean reached for him, but Miles moved away. She pulled her hand back. "I wanted, no, needed, to be your sister. I thought it would help me find Mara. I was so afraid, Miles. You can't imagine. She was obsessed over you. You were...are...her favorite movie star. You have power and connections I don't. I didn't have anywhere else to turn. You have to believe me—"

Miles stiffened at the desperation in her voice. "I can't trust you, Jean. You can't stay here anymore." Her panicked look tore at his heart, but he continued. "I'll do what I can to help you find your daughter, but that's where our relationship ends. You'll have to find another...resource."

"What about the premiere? I have to be there. You've got to let me go, Miles." Tears streamed down her cheeks. "I need to find my baby. You don't understand—"

"You can come to the premiere, but that's the end of it. If she doesn't show up there, then you won't have any other choice but to call the police."

"Miles…please, listen to me—"

He grabbed the container from the microwave and walked out of the kitchen, Jean's plea echoing in the hall behind him.

Yuri hurried through the parking garage beneath Greg's office. He didn't want to be late for this meeting. Greg had called and told him all was forgiven. That he needed him to stop by for a briefing about the girl. He smoothed his hair down with his hand before he opened the door and stepped into the emergency stairwell. The feel of his new gun snug against his back gave him more confidence than he normally would have in this situation.

Yuri knew he was taking a chance meeting with Greg, but he also knew he was fucked six ways to Sunday if he stayed in L.A. His uncle Vladimir had assured him of that. Even though he was family, Vladimir said, Yuri would no longer be able to enjoy the safety of his uncle's extensive criminal network. Not if he was on the powerful trafficker's shit list. Those kinds of problems tended to bleed over into blood feuds and Vlad had no desire to go to war with the "shit-heel rat-fuck," as he so delicately put it.

There was also the other, delusional problem of Yuri being unable to let go of his dream of living large in the City of Angels. It was his destiny, of that he was certain. Greg would listen to his side of the story and give him another chance. He had to.

Yuri took the first three flights of stairs two at a time. By the time he'd reached the fourth floor, he was considerably winded and slowed down to try and catch his breath. A door slammed above him and he jumped. He'd never known anyone to take the stairs. Not in this building.

He pulled his gun out of his waistband and warily climbed the stairs to the fifth floor, his eyes riveted above him on the stairwell. A shadow crossed the lone light bulb illuminating the sixth floor entry; the sound of footsteps accompanied by whistling echoed in the passageway. Yuri stopped and thought about heading back down as they drew closer.

He swiveled and placed his foot on the stair below him, intending to return to his car when he heard Ned's voice.

"Hey, Yuri. Long time no see."

He turned to see him standing in the stairwell above him, a smile on his face. Yuri relaxed his death grip on the gun and shoved it back into his waistband. He started to climb toward him.

"Greg called me to come in today."

"Yeah. About that. Remember when you said no one takes the stairs in L.A.?" Ned asked.

Yuri hesitated, his hand on the metal railing. "Yes?"

"Well, I mentioned that to Greg and he thought it would be a fitting place." Ned had his hand behind his back.

"For what?" Yuri asked, reaching for his gun.

"For you to die."

Yuri caught the glint of Ned's semiautomatic as he pulled out his own and fired.

Ned fell forward, tumbling down the stairwell, and came to a rest at Yuri's feet. Not waiting for the response sure to follow from the gunshot, he flew down the steps, jumped over the handrail and landed with a thud on the concrete landing before he exploded through the safety door into the parking garage.

CHAPTER THIRTY-TWO

LEINE SNAPPED THE GUN MAGAZINE back into place. Additional ammunition went into the cargo pockets of her pants. She slipped Mara's picture into her jacket pocket, along with a copy of Selena's mug shot. If Miles still decided to ignore the obvious after she showed him the picture, then she would give up trying to convince him of the woman's guilt. The only reason she could come up with for his behavior was that as an actor he had an extraordinary ability to ignore reality. A dangerous trait, though one that apparently worked well on film.

Just not in life.

Not only did she need to keep Selena in her sights, Leine had to be ready to move quickly to help Mara if she showed at the event. Her main goal was to retrieve the young girl and get her to safety. Her secondary and tertiary goals were to immobilize Selena and/or the traffickers, and to keep Miles out of harm's way.

She'd already run through possible scenarios but discarded most of them. In her experience, predetermined events rarely played out as expected. Take a crowd of people, add critical stressors and you had the elements for a major cluster. She would have to respond rapidly to emerging conditions unencumbered by false expectations.

She picked up the leather bag with the guns she'd taken from her apartment, took one last look around her hotel room to make sure she'd gotten everything, then slipped out the door.

A few minutes later, she exited the stairwell into the parking garage and headed for her new ride, a nondescript sedan with a supercharged Hemi motor. She scanned the area for anything out of place before dropping the bag on the garage floor near the trunk. She opened a side pocket, pulled out an angled mirror with a telescoping rod and ran it underneath the car, looking for explosives.

Satisfied there was nothing attached to the underside of the car, she carefully opened the hood, first getting a visual with a flashlight, then running her fingertips around the edges to make sure there were no tripwires or pressure sensitive triggers installed while she was in the hotel room. She went through the drill each time she'd been away from her car.

Better late than dead.

After she investigated under the hood, paying particular attention to the wires leading to the starter, she did the same check on her trunk. Finding nothing suspicious, she opened it and placed the bag containing the weapons under a tarp. With every movement, the Kevlar she was wearing put pressure on her bruised ribs and she had to catch her breath. At least the vest stabilized her torso. That, and a shot of Toradol helped her push past the pain.

Except for when she forgot about the injury and didn't guard her movements. Then the pain took her breath away.

She knew the theater's layout, had visited the area that morning and memorized the position of every column, garbage can, doorway and building in case things went sideways.

Leine added another primary objective to her mental checklist: to avoid gunfire in the populated venue. That wouldn't be easy if the traffickers turned up.

She checked her watch. An hour and a half before the premiere. Time enough to work her way through security in order to speak to Miles. If that didn't work, she was prepared to slip the photograph to his bodyguard and ask that it be delivered to the actor with a note.

She closed the trunk and went over the rest of the car before she came back to the driver's side and opened the door to get in.

The noise wasn't loud. More like a faint scrape followed by a tiny shift in atmosphere, as though someone or something had moved behind her. Leine stiffened, straining to hear. She pivoted in the direction of the sound, hand moving to the nine millimeter in her shoulder holster. She drew her gun and waited, staring into the darkness of the garage, but saw nothing.

Blood thudded in her ears. She shrugged her shoulders and cracked her neck to the side to ease the tension. Still wired, she returned the gun to the holster and climbed into the car.

Leine emerged from the garage, turned right onto the shaded, tree-lined side street and headed for the freeway. Almost immediately, a dark-colored Mercedes Benz appeared in her rearview mirror. She took the next right, watching to see if the vehicle followed her. It drove past, continuing down the other street. She turned left twice and proceeded on a different route to the freeway.

Stopped at a traffic light, she scanned the area for the Mercedes. Other than a couple of parked cars, there weren't any other vehicles in sight. The light turned green and she drove through the intersection. Two blocks later, she noticed a flash of black in her periphery. The dark-colored car barreled toward her on her right. She slammed the accelerator to the floor. The sedan shot forward and gathered speed. The Mercedes tracked her, coming up on the rear of the car, dangerously close to the bumper.

Leine braced herself as the other car surged forward and clipped the back corner of the sedan. *Not again.* She yanked the steering wheel to the left and skidded around a corner, the Mercedes matching her move. It stayed with her on every turn. Instinctively, Leine mapped out a route in her head that took them away from heavily populated residential areas. The end result would put them in a semi-deserted neighborhood inhabited by the occasional tweaker in the few remaining ramshackle homes. Addicts tended to stay inside during the day.

The person in the other car had to be another one of Eric's operatives. It was as though the driver intuited her every move and matched her maneuver for maneuver. He was good, she'd give him that. Rather than intimidate, the realization energized her. Taking him out would send a strong message to her ex-boss that whatever he tried, she'd counter. He'd no doubt work to pin this on her, too, so she was screwed either way. What did she have to lose?

She entered the neighborhood with her senses on hyper-alert. The sedan screamed past the first home, a two-story wreck with peeling blue paint and no intact windows, the Mercedes a hair's breadth behind her. The vacant lot at the end of the avenue came into focus and Leine reached for the hand brake. She waited until the car cleared the last house, then wrenched the lever up and rammed the brake pedal to the floor.

The sedan skidded into the turn, kicking up dust and rocks, and for a split-second obscured the other car's visual. As soon as the car stopped moving, Leine kicked open the door, dropped to the ground and took cover behind the rear wheel well, gun aimed over the trunk at the other car.

The driver of the Mercedes ducked as the bullets from Leine's semiautomatic smashed into the Mercedes' windshield. Ignoring the searing pain in her side, Leine opened the trunk, grabbed the Uzi, and pocketed a grenade before the shooter had the chance to crawl out the passenger side. The torrent of bullets from the submachine gun finished the job on the windows, shattering the glass and scattering it everywhere.

She continued to fire in short bursts from her position behind the car, pockmarking the Mercedes. When she dropped to a crouch to reload, she expected return fire. It didn't happen.

"Who sent you?" Leine called out, as she snapped a fresh magazine into the grip of the Uzi. Her voice echoed in the emptiness of the lot. There was no response. She tried to slow her breathing, which proved difficult. Every inhalation was torture. "I know you're one of Eric's errand boys. Come out and show yourself. Or are you afraid to engage the enemy?"

At the sound of rocks scattering, she stood and aimed, still protected by the car, waiting for signs of the other gunman. A low cough floated across the expanse between the two cars.

"It appears I've underestimated you."

Leine froze at the voice. *You're shitting me.* "Eric?"

"The one and only."

Leine squinted, trying to get a bead on where he was in relation to the Mercedes. His shadow was barely visible near the other car's rear wheel. Not a clear shot. She needed to change her position. White-hot hatred for the man behind the Mercedes flowed through her, mixing with the adrenaline. She frowned in annoyance at the slight shake in her left hand. *Control, Leine.*

"Decided to do the job yourself, eh?" she called, her voice cool and even. "I imagine losing the last guy you sent after me was a huge disappointment. Really, Eric," Leine made a *tsking* sound. "He wasn't your best. I'm more than a little peeved you didn't think enough of me to send Barbara or Rolf."

"And why would I send my best to take out a rogue agent? Especially one who's obviously rusty."

"Who says I'm rusty? And why the hell didn't you try to take me out in the garage? I mean, it worked out well for me, but honestly, it would have been better odds." She paused, then added, "Maybe you're the rusty one."

"In your younger days you wouldn't have missed."

Leine stretched her neck to the side before answering. "In my younger days, I would've gotten a full dossier on my target and had time to plan." She slid down behind the car, leaving just enough of herself exposed in order to get a good shot if he moved.

"Yeah, those were good times, huh, Leine? God, the money was fantastic. I would've cut you in on the deals if you'd asked."

This time Leine laughed, but there was no mirth. "Is that why you had me kill Carlos and fed lies to my daughter? So I'd be willing to look the other way? You're five steps below a mercenary, Eric. At least mercenaries admit to having an allegiance only to money. You cloak yourself in the fabric of patriotism." Her spike of anger had leveled and she welcomed the clarity it brought. "I have to say that did a number on my head for a while, but when you took the most precious thing I'd ever known and crushed it without a thought for me or those I loved, I finally got it. That's when I left."

"And took Carlos' files with you."

"A girl's gotta have a little security. Leaving the Agency alive wasn't an option."

Leine peered over the hood at the sound of gravel shifting beside his car. Why hadn't he made his move yet? She didn't have all damn day. "Looks like we're at a standoff. What do you want to do?"

He paused for a moment before answering, his ragged breathing audible in the silent afternoon. "It appears one of your bullets found a home in my shoulder and I'm having trouble raising my arm." He coughed again. "This isn't a fair fight, Leine. How about we each go our separate ways, come back and do this another time?"

Sure. "I don't think so, Eric. But while I've got you here, can you answer something for me? You've been working pretty hard to pin those three murders on me, and it appeared to be working. Why try to kill me now? Unless..." Leine paused before continuing. The answer was obvious. "Did your boss have a problem with the second set of files, Eric?" Her question was met with silence. "Well, damn. They must have finally made it through whatever firewall you set up. With me dead, there's no way to verify the origin of the documents. You'd have a much easier time convincing your bosses the file is the creation of a deranged agent bent on revenge. All you'd have to say is that I came after you and you had to kill me."

"It's not like you have a lot to live for," he said, his oily tone sliding over her like a viscous poison. "Your daughter doesn't need you—she's on her own. Been that way for some time. Quite the independent woman. And, Mr. Tall Dark Detective sure as hell won't jeopardize his career to be with an ex-assassin. A man who, by the way, reminds me a lot of Carlos. Is that why you were attracted to him?"

"Fuck off." *He'd been watching.*

"Touchy, touchy. Did I hit a nerve? How does your resume play in the boudoir? I'll bet he has a hard time getting it up. I mean, you *killed* people for a living—and were quite good at it, too. Doesn't that give him pause? Especially since he took an oath to uphold the law."

Leine clenched her jaw in an effort to stop the sarcastic comment that sprang to her lips. She didn't need to sink to his level. What she needed was to end this, now.

"Leave Santiago Jensen and my daughter out of it. I wonder whose budget paid for the surveillance? Neither of them are official Agency targets, right?" She waited for an answer, but none came. "This is between you and me, Eric. Let's finish up. I need to be somewhere."

More silence.

Leine skirted the front corner of the sedan, keeping her eye on the shadow next to the rear wheel well. She debated whether to use the grenade, but at the last minute decided against it. It would have made her feel better, yes, but local law enforcement wouldn't be able to ignore the explosion like they could gunfire in this section of town. As it was, there'd be questions when they recovered the Mercedes. Questions she wouldn't be around to answer.

She crossed the gap between the two vehicles and stopped near the trunk of the Mercedes. Holding the gun in front of her, she eased around the car.

Eric sat slumped against the wheel, breathing heavily, his black suit coat skewed around his chest, one leg bent at an angle, the other stretched in front of him. His reddish-blond hair was slicked back from his boyish, clean-shaven face, giving him the appearance of a much younger man, except for the lines around his hazel-colored eyes. Leine's gaze stopped at where he'd shoved his left fist into his armpit in an attempt to stanch the flow of blood now saturating his shirt.

"You weren't lying," she said. "Except about me missing."

Eric's smile looked closer to a grimace. "Yeah. Can you beat that?" He glanced down at the gunshot wound, then squinted up at Leine. "You're looking well."

"Thanks." Leine kicked his gun out of his reach and pointed hers at his head.

"You might as well shoot. I'm dead, anyway." Eric's breathing had become more ragged and he winced as he shifted position. "Can you do it soon? This hurts like a mother." He eyed the grenade. "You always did like explosions." His attempt at laughter turned into a hacking cough. Leine could tell it cost him.

"Not enough to end your suffering."

Eric leaned his head back and looked at the sky. The skin on his face looked gray, his life ebbing. "Oh, c'mon, Leine. For old time's sake? I'd consider it an honor. Dispatched by the great Leine Basso."

"Flattery never worked on me before. Why try now?" Leine bent down and placed the grenade in the hand of his bad arm. His fingers curled around it, his palm against the safety lever. He closed his eyes, lips contorted in a smile.

"Say hello to the Frenchman," Leine said, and walked back to her car.

She'd driven halfway down the block when the explosion cracked through the neighborhood, the sound ricocheting off the wall of a nearby home. Pieces of twisted metal arced in the air and fell to the ground. Leine slowed the car and watched as the Mercedes burned, spewing black smoke into the sky. The horizon flickered like a mirage from the heat. The front door of one of the houses swung open and a cadaverous woman with hollow eyes rimmed by dark circles walked onto the decrepit porch, blinking in the sunlight, confusion evident on her face.

Leine stared at the flames for a few seconds more, then proceeded to the end of the street and turned right.

She didn't look back.

CHAPTER THIRTY-THREE

MILES STARED OUT THE WINDOW of the limo as gray clouds gathered in the distance, thinking about his life. The afternoon had turned unseasonably cool and the threat of rain put him in a pensive mood. He thought of the people who would come to see him, especially the kids, standing outside in shitty weather while he said some words and shook a few hands. Jesus, what was he doing? The fame and money had been fun for a while, but he'd felt alive for the first time in his life when he thought he had a family to care for. Like he was part of something larger than himself.

Otherwise, what the hell was the point? He could only spend so much money. If he quit making movies right now, he'd have more than enough to live, and live well until he died, no matter how old he got. He looked over at Jean, sitting on the other side of the limo, thumbing through a magazine. She'd been silent since they left the house. Miles didn't try to strike up a conversation with her. There was nothing to say. He'd allowed her to come along this last time. After that, she was on her own.

His chest tightened as he fought back the hurt and anger. Her deceit was unforgivable. Miles thought about Jarvis, and how he'd let Miles down that night at the bar when the two assholes picked a fight and he'd disappeared. Jean's betrayal cut much deeper. Sure, he'd considered Jarvis family, but he'd believed Jean was his blood.

Miles smoothed the lapels of his suit as the limo pulled to the curb in front of the theater amid a throng of screaming fans. He glanced at Jean as she checked her makeup in her compact mirror and shook his head.

"You can ride around and come in through the back. I don't want you on the carpet with me." He cast a meaningful glance at his new bodyguard, Thad. Thad lifted his chin in acknowledgement.

Jean stopped primping and nodded, her eyes downcast. "Sure, Miles. I appreciate you letting me come to the premiere. I know Mara's going to show up. I can feel it."

"I hope so, for her sake." Miles pressed a button and the glass divider between the driver and the back of the limo lowered. "Can you take Jean around to the rear entrance, Joe?" Joe nodded. Miles turned and, without a backward glance at Jean, pasted on a broad smile as he climbed out to greet his fans, with Thad close behind.

As the car glided by the crowd gathered in front of the theater, Selena took her phone from her pocketbook, touched the screen and held it to her ear, waiting for the other party to answer.

"We're here. He wants me to come in through the back. What should I do?" she asked when they answered.

189

"Get out in the crowd and mingle. Keep a low profile, but be ready for her. We'll take care of the rest." The background noise suggested the caller was riding in a car. "And, Selena? Remember, we're watching you."

"When can I see her—"

The line went dead.

She stared at the phone as a feeling of dread crept up her spine. What if they didn't keep their word? A part of her had died when they told her what they planned to do with Amy if she didn't cooperate. She would have done anything to get her back. They'd assured her the two of them would be reunited after the premiere.

Now Miles didn't trust her, making everything that much harder. All the time she'd spent memorizing the details about Miles' and Mara's lives, all the studying she'd done, was for nothing. All because of Leine Basso. She'd tried to alleviate the woman's suspicions, thought she'd done a good job, but then they'd had that argument in the bathroom at the Briar Cliff when Leine pulled a gun on her. Though it had petrified her, the incident helped cement her relationship with Miles. It also made an enemy of Leine.

She hadn't seen the DNA results coming. Although she'd known the test was a certainty, Greg had assured her she'd be out of Miles' life before it became an issue. She'd mistakenly thought they'd have to ask her permission, or at the very least inform her of their intentions.

The limo rounded the corner and drew even with the back of the theater. She checked her makeup once more in the mirror as Joe got out and came around to open the door. She took a deep breath and climbed out, Joe's hand helping to steady her as she stood. A lone paparazzi waiting nearby came forward, but when he saw she wasn't anyone famous he slipped back into position. A uniformed cop stood sentry near the door. It was a far cry from the explosion of camera flashes and people trying to get her attention when she was with Miles.

The life she'd been pretending to live was now coming to an end. She didn't know what would happen if Mara didn't show up and try to get to Miles. Time was running out and she would no longer have any influence, would be back to living at the whim of the brutal man she'd just spoken with on the phone. She'd have ended her life long ago, if it wasn't for the chance of being able to save her younger sister.

She'd have to make sure things went right this time.

Miles smiled and shook hands with the crowd, searching every face. He'd given Thad a head's up and showed him Mara's picture, although he found himself wishing Leine was there with him instead of the silent blond man with the crew cut who shadowed his every move. At least Leine had called him on his bullshit. True, he went ahead and usually did what he wanted, but at least he knew she took an interest in his well-being. Thad was too distant. When Miles tried to strike up a conversation, he gave short, curt answers. The guy was a one-word wonder.

Thad nudged him in the side. Miles finished signing a kid's program and turned to see what he wanted. Leine watched them from behind the red velvet rope. Relief washed through him as he walked over to talk to her.

"You need to see this," Leine said, handing him an envelope.

Miles opened it and slid the picture out. He glanced at Leine. "A mug shot of Jean?"

"Her name's not Jean, Miles."

He looked back at the picture. "Selena Fullerton?"

"I ran her fingerprints."

He could feel her stare at him as he processed the new information. "Mara's not her daughter, is she?"

Leine shook her head. "No. I'm pretty sure she's working for the traffickers."

Rico Pallini hurried down the aisle toward him. When he caught sight of Leine, his eyes narrowed. He stopped short and put his hand on Miles' elbow in an attempt to direct him back to his fans, but Miles shrugged it off.

"What can we do? She's here," Miles asked Leine. Feelings of betrayal mixed with fear for Mara's safety rushed through him. He'd let one of the traffickers come to the premiere, putting Mara's life in danger.

"Who's here?" Rico demanded.

"Where is she?" Leine asked, ignoring Rico's question.

"I told her to come through the back. Leine—" Miles stopped for a moment and took a deep breath. "I'm sorry I didn't believe you before. You were right."

"Right about what? Who the hell are you talking about?" Rico's complexion had turned a deep red. He leaned over to whisper in Miles' ear. "This isn't the time to be dealing with anything but your adoring fans, so buck up and get moving."

"Give me a minute, okay, Rico? I'm talking to Leine."

Rico scowled at Leine but was all smiles as he stepped toward the crowd to keep them occupied.

Miles slipped Selena's picture into his pocket. "What should I do if Mara shows up?"

"If you see her, make a scene. Make it hard for them to grab her without being noticed. I'll be somewhere in the crowd, watching." She turned to leave.

Rico reappeared at Miles' side. "You gotta move, Miles. They're getting restless. And Vicki from *Entertainment All the Time!* is waiting to ask you a few questions." He indicated the reporter a few yards away on the red carpet, speaking with one of Miles' co-stars.

"I'll talk with you later, okay Leine?"

Leine nodded and stepped back into the crowd. People who'd been standing behind her surged forward to fill the empty gap in front of Miles. He automatically took one of the programs thrust at him and signed his name.

"What the hell was that about? I thought you never wanted to talk to her again," Rico said, his voice low.

Miles handed back the fan's program and accepted another as he answered. "Jean's not who she says she is, Rico."

"Leine tried to tell you that before. You said you didn't care, that you still wanted to help her. What's changed?"

Miles pulled the photograph from his pocket. "This."

Rico glanced at the photo. "Yeah, so? It's a mug shot of Jean. She told you about her DUI."

Miles turned to look at Rico. "Read the name under the picture."

Rico stiffened, his expression registering confusion. "Selena Fullerton?" He followed Miles as he moved up the aisle, shaking hands and greeting his fans. "Are you telling me Jean—I mean, Selena's not Jean?" Miles nodded. Rico's eyes widened. "You're kidding me, right?"

"No."

Rico rubbed his hand over his face. "Did you say she was here? Where's she now?"

"Coming in the back," Miles said over his shoulder, still signing autographs. "Be careful, Rico. We don't know what she's capable of."

"Right. I'll take care of it, Miles," he said. "You keep working the crowd."

Miles nodded. "Yeah. It's what I do best, right, Rico?"

CHAPTER THIRTY-FOUR

LEINE SLIPPED THROUGH THE THRONG of screaming fans, searching each young girl's face for Mara. If she could clone herself, she'd find Selena and immobilize her. At this point, finding Mara and getting her to safety was her first objective. If she left to find Selena and missed Mara she'd never forgive herself.

She headed toward the steps of the building next to the theater to get a visual of the area. The height enabled her to see both the crowd and watch Miles' progress toward the theater. Large posters announcing the movie acted as a backdrop where his co-stars had gathered at the entrance, waiting for him to join them before heading in for photos.

A man with a shaved head caught her eye. He looked out of place in the crowd of younger people and their mothers. Granted, there were a few men, probably fathers, in attendance, but most of them looked like they belonged with someone. Leine watched the man to see if he spoke to anyone, but he appeared to be alone.

Miles wrapped his interview with the woman reporter from *Entertainment All the Time!* and began to make his way up the red carpet past the crowd to join his co-stars. If Mara was there, now would be the time she'd show herself.

Miles smiled and waved for the cameras as he joined the group. He shook hands with each of his co-stars and hugged his leading lady, all the while posing for the fans.

Out of the corner of her eye, Leine noticed Selena making her way through the crowd. The man with the shaved head changed his position so that he was only a few feet from where Selena stood. Scanning the area, Leine spotted two more men who didn't fit the demographics.

There was still no sign of Mara. Leine slipped down the steps and skirted the large crowd on the far side of the red carpet, edging closer to Selena and the other men. The man with the shaved head wore a bulky black leather coat, as did the other two. Leine held off, not wanting to spook any of them, and kept her head down in case Selena looked her way. Seeing Leine would set off alarm bells and could cause any traffickers that were there to scatter. She wanted them where she could see them.

Miles cracked a joke and the people standing nearby laughed. Somewhere in the back, a little girl screamed that she loved Miles, which set off a cacophony of screams and whistles. The man with the shaved head frowned as he searched the crowd. The wind whipped up and the tent that had been erected above the red carpet billowed. A splattering of rain drops fell on those unlucky enough to be in the open.

Selena's glance darted from person to person. The light rain turned into a downpour and people covered their heads with their programs, turning the crowd into a sea of paper. If Mara was there, it'd be like trying to find a needle in a haystack.

Leine kept her eye on Selena. Mara would likely avoid the obvious thugs in the crowd. She wouldn't necessarily pay attention to a woman, unless she had recognized her at the restaurant. Leine closed the distance separating her from Selena and stepped behind a couple with their daughter when she glanced her way.

The man with the shaved head spotted Selena and started toward her, his mouth set in a grim line. Selena didn't notice him at first, but as he drew nearer she turned and saw him. Her face paled and she moved in the opposite direction as she continued to watch the crowd. *Why is she so scared of him, if she's working with the traffickers?* Maybe there's another explanation, Leine thought.

Then Leine saw her. The sea of programs parted as Mara inched her way through the crowd toward the theater entrance, directly in Selena's path. Leine lost her for a moment, then located her again. Mara was now within several feet of Selena, although she hadn't seen her yet. Leine struggled to push through the throng, but only managed to gain a few feet before being shoved backward. She wiped a shock of wet hair off her face, irritation replaced by fear for Mara's safety.

Pinned between several screaming fans, the man with the shaved head raised his arms and waved at Selena to get her attention. Selena saw him and scanned the crowd to see what he was pointing at. She caught a glimpse of Leine and a look of alarm crossed her features. The man with the shaved head followed her gaze and immediately headed toward Leine.

Mara managed to make her way to the velvet rope next to the red carpet and now stood within a foot of Selena. She waved her hands and jumped up and down, straining to get Miles' attention. Selena's gaze settled on the young girl. Recognition lit her face and she reached down and latched onto Mara's upper arm. Surprised, Mara started to scream, but Selena clamped her hand across her mouth. Mara fought, twisting and slapping at her captor as Selena dragged her through the crowd. Leine tried to fight through the mass of people, but for every step forward she was pushed back two. Mara struggled to hang back, but Selena was too strong and the crowd too thick for her to break free.

Leine pressed through the mob, keeping Selena and Mara in sight. The pain in her side had become a dull, constant ache, interspersed with sharp jolts of pain when someone in the crowd jostled against her too hard. As she reached the edge of the crowd, something hard pressed against her back, next to her kidney. She inhaled sharply and pivoted, coming face-to-face with the man with the shaved head. His dark eyes narrowed as he shoved a gun with a suppressor into Leine's abdomen.

"Let them go," he said, his voice a low growl.

Her reflexes took over and Leine slammed her hand against his wrist and stepped to the side. The gun went off, the bullet burying itself in the concrete. No one noticed. The screaming fans obliterated the muffled sound. She delivered a quick jab to his throat with her right hand and followed the move by ramming the heel of her left into his face. He dropped the gun to the ground, grabbing his now bloody nose with one hand and clawed at his throat with the other as he struggled to take a breath. Ignoring the pain in her side, she rammed her knee into his groin and he went down. A woman dressed in capris and high heels stared in horror at the bloodied man lying in a fetal position on the sidewalk and backed away. In a panic, she looked toward the theater and screamed for a cop. Leine seized the opportunity and picked up the gun, shoved it under her jacket and took off running in the direction she'd seen Jean and Mara disappear.

She rounded the corner of the theater and slowed to a fast walk, zipping her jacket closed to conceal the gun as she came to the alley. The squall stopped as quickly as it started, leaving several puddles in its wake. Leine entered the side street, one hand on the vest above her bruised ribs, her breath shallow. With her back to the wall, she searched the area.

There was no one in the alley. She sprinted to the end and searched the cross street both directions. There were a few people walking along the sidewalk, but no sign of Selena or Mara. She made her way to the back entrance. The uniformed cop stationed at the back door watched her, his face like stone.

"Did you see a woman and a young girl come by here?" she called to him.

He shook his head.

She'd lost them.

Leine returned to the parking lot where she'd parked her car, her frustration growing. She was going to have to go back to Vladimir and ask him to help her find Greg. She doubted Yuri was still alive, knowing it was only a matter of time before Greg's thugs found him.

Going to Vlad was the only way she would be able to track the trafficker down. Knowing him, he'd extract an even bigger trade this time. But, if she found Greg, she might have a chance of finding Mara. The man who'd purchased her was local. That meant she wouldn't be leaving the country. It gave Leine time to find her, but not long. If she didn't get to her soon...

Leine refused to think about what would happen to the young girl if she didn't find her in the next few hours. She pulled out her keys and hurried down the aisle to her car, slowing when she realized someone was leaning against the hood, his back to her. He was tall and thin and wore a brown wool cap and a black quilted coat. She unzipped her jacket and pulled out her gun, and crept up behind him until the barrel was within inches of the back of his head.

"I have a gun pointed at your head, so don't make any impulsive moves," Leine said in a low voice. The man stiffened, then lifted both hands to show he had no weapon and slowly turned around.

It was Yuri.

Chapter Thirty-Five

PLEASE, DON'T SHOOT. I HAVE come to help you."
Yuri's eyes darted nervously back and forth,
checking the lot behind Leine.

Leine lowered the gun so it wasn't visible to passersby
but kept it trained on Yuri. "How the hell did you know
this was my car?"

"I was waiting across the street and saw you park. I
knew you'd come here to look for the girl."

Leine scanned the parking lot, but didn't see anyone
else close by. "You can explain later why you're still alive.
There's no time. Your compatriots have the girl. We need
to go."

He slammed his fist on the car. "I *knew* she would be
here. It was the last place she could see Fournier before
he left for Europe."

"Get in." Leine unlocked the doors, climbed in and
started the car. Yuri opened the door and slid in the
passenger's seat. "Where's Greg's office?" she asked,
grimacing as she twisted in her seat and backed out of the
parking space.

"Are you all right?" Yuri asked, watching her.

"I'm fine. Where are we going?"

He took a deep breath. "Sixth floor of the Brandon Building on Ventura Boulevard."

Leine glanced at him before she drove out of the parking lot. "You'd best be telling the truth."

"You'll see. I'm good on my word. Thank you for not killing me."

"Don't thank me yet."

They made good time despite the wet roads and traffic. Leine pulled over to the curb a few buildings down from the Brandon Building and parked. She checked the chamber in her gun and, satisfied there was plenty of ammunition, screwed a suppressor onto the barrel. She preferred to use her own weapon, rather than that of the trafficker she'd just nailed. Yuri's knee kept time with some syncopated beat only in his head.

"Nervous, Yuri?" Leine looked pointedly at his leg. He stopped jiggling his knee. "Before I go in there, I need you to tell me why you're helping me. If I don't like the answer, things will go badly for you."

Yuri nodded. The tip of his tongue snaked out and wet his lips. "Greg called and said everything was fine, that he needed me back. Being a fool, I believed my good fortune and came to meet with him. He sent someone to kill me. He is dead and now I am here."

"And I'm the only one you know who can protect you." She glanced at the office building. "I'm surprised you're willing to come back to this place."

Yuri shook his head. "I have given you the information you requested. You have no more need of me. I will wait here for you."

204

"I'm afraid not, Yuri. You're coming with me. The more the merrier."

The look on Yuri's face told her that he hadn't lied, at least about this being Greg's office. He definitely didn't want to come along for the ride. She didn't know what she'd find, if anything, but she had to try. She couldn't just give up on Mara. Not when she'd been so close. She opened her door and got out. With obvious reluctance, Yuri did the same.

"Do you recognize any of the cars?" she asked, indicating the building's parking lot.

He shook his head. "No. Greg drives a black Navigator, and it's not in his usual spot. It's possible he could be parked in the garage below, but he doesn't like it there. He prefers to park outside."

"Then he won't be any help finding what we're looking for." Leine assumed Greg was delivering Mara to the buyer personally. It wouldn't look good if he lost her again.

"Are you going to call the cops?" Yuri asked.

"Why? Got some outstanding warrants, Yuri?" His look was enough to tell her he did. "Look, I haven't got anything definitive to tell them. Greg's not here, and we don't know where they took Mara. I'm working on a hunch. The LAPD doesn't roll on a hunch."

His features relaxed. "I know the buyer is a…how do you say it? A big honcho? I also heard he lives in Los Angeles."

It fit with what Lou told her. "How does Greg keep his files? Paper or electronic?"

"I think electronic. He is always working on a computer."

"What kind of security does he have?"

Yuri squeezed his eyes shut as he thought. "There is a camera in the lobby by the elevator, one in the elevator and one outside the front door. At the door to the offices, you wait for someone to buzz you in."

Leine walked to the trunk of her car and opened it. Rooting around in the bag, she found what she was looking for and pocketed the items, then closed the trunk. "Time to move." They crossed the street and walked toward the building. "What about the rear entrance?" she asked, as she pulled on a pair of latex gloves.

Yuri shrugged. "I don't know. I never used it."

As they approached the building, Leine noticed a small security camera above and slightly to the right. She pulled a small black box from her pocket and handed it to Yuri.

"Aim it at the camera and hold this button down. Keep holding it until I say stop."

Yuri nodded and did what she told him to do. The amber light on top of the camera blinked off. She walked to the door and tested it to see if it was unlocked. It was. She opened it and motioned for Yuri to follow.

"Do you want me to continue to press this button?" he asked.

"Did I tell you to stop?"

"No." Yuri's face grew pink. He backed into the building behind her, keeping the device aimed at the camera.

"Stop," Leine said. Yuri dropped his arm and handed the jammer to her. The light on the camera reappeared. Avoiding the elevator, he led the way to the stairwell and they started to climb. A dark stain covered a section of the landing near the fifth floor, which Yuri carefully skirted. Leine ignored it and stopped at the door on the sixth.

Yuri cracked it open and checked the hallway, then motioned for her to follow him. He was visibly sweating and repeatedly looked over his shoulder to check behind them. Leine put her hand on his arm to calm him, and he jumped a foot. She was rethinking her idea of bringing him along to get her inside. She could have scrambled the lock, but she didn't trust the Ukrainian and wanted to be sure they were actually going to Greg's office.

Yuri stopped at the end of the corridor near a door with a card reader next to the handle. No sign indicated whose office it was. He glanced down the hallway one more time and turned to Leine.

"This is where I press the button, Greg asks who is there and then he buzzes me in."

"Press the button," Leine said.

Yuri's breathing resembled that of a dog after a particularly long hunt. "What if he's in there?" Yuri whispered, his anxiety palpable.

She slid her gun from the holster and stood to the side. "Then he's going to be very surprised."

Yuri's hand shook as he pressed the button. Moments passed. There was no response. He let out his breath, relief washing over his face. It was quickly replaced by a look of concern. "But how will you get inside?"

Leine pulled a slim device about the size of a credit card from her pocket and inserted it into the card reader. The red light changed to green and there was a click as the lock disengaged. Leine turned the handle and opened the door. Yuri followed her in and closed the door behind them.

"That's a very handy device."

"Where's his office?" she asked, ignoring his comment.

Yuri pointed down the short hall. "Past the conference room, second door on the left. I can show you."

Leine shook her head. "I need you to go to where the monitors are and watch to make sure no one comes."

"Ah. Of course. I will do this." Yuri hurried past the reception area and turned right down a second hallway.

Leine walked past the conference room and into Greg's office, and went over to his desk to turn on his computer. While she waited for it to boot up, she crossed the floor to a gray metal file cabinet marked *Talent* that stood against the wall and opened each drawer. She quickly scanned the files in the hopes that something would catch her attention.

She was amazed at how thorough the records were. File after file had pictures of women attached to comprehensive reports detailing their height, weight, eye and hair color, age, date of birth, home towns, names of family members, everything. However, as far as Leine could tell, there were no women listed under the age of eighteen. There was also no indication of where the women were now.

Leine closed the last drawer and returned to the computer. The screen prompted her for a password. Leine reached in her pocket and took out another electronic device, this one a small gray box with a USB connector, and plugged it into a port on the monitor. She waited a few moments as the screen changed to a black background with several lines of code. Leine typed a command and the device quietly went to work, creating then discarding various combinations of passwords at lightning speed.

Using a jeweler's loop, she peered at the keyboard for signs of wear on the keypad. A series of ten keys appeared to have been used more frequently than the rest. She typed in another command and a second dialogue box materialized with space for her to input them. This second program ran alongside the first one she'd activated and worked specifically on combinations containing those specific keys.

As she waited for the program to finish, she checked in and around the desk, crouching underneath to get a visual in case Greg decided to hide anything noteworthy there. He hadn't. She stood and moved to the middle of the room, then pivoted three-hundred-and-sixty degrees, looking to see if anything stood out that she might need to investigate further.

The device beeped softly and Leine returned to the desk. The password had been determined and the screen now displayed Greg's desktop. She disconnected the hacking device and put it inside her pocket before clicking through the files. Each document she opened appeared to be related to income from a cover talent agency. Names, dates and places were linked to several of the women whose files were in the cabinet, and in most instances they appeared to reference legitimate businesses.

Leine scanned the full list of documents on the hard drive, keying in on one titled *Production,* which she opened. The document had two columns. One listed twelve gmail addresses, all beginning with the word Gatekeeper_ followed by two letters. A second column listed random letters and symbols directly across from the emails, obviously passwords. Leine brought up the internet and began to methodically check each one. The first five had no messages in the inboxes. She checked the drafts and deleted folders as well as sent messages, but they were all empty.

Gatekeeper_MQ had nothing in the inbox or the sent folders, but there was a message in drafts. She clicked on it and read the single sentence.

88838 Mulholland Drive. Rear entrance. Gate code: brothers1. SE.

Leine looked at the date: it had been composed that morning. Her heart beat faster as she realized there was a high probability the MQ stood for Mara Quigg, with the address indicating where they'd taken her. She plugged a flash drive into one of the USB ports, copied the content of Greg's hard disk and then closed out of everything and shut down the computer.

She walked around the desk, intending to leave, but stopped when she heard the front door open and close. Leine reached for her gun and crept toward the door. Either Yuri just left, or they had company.

Her back to the wall, Leine stood still and listened. She caught the unmistakable sound of footsteps falling on carpet, coming toward her. She waited until the person walked past the door and then stepped into the hallway.

A small, gray-haired woman dressed in a white t-shirt, navy colored stretch pants and tennis shoes gasped and put her hand to her chest when she saw Leine.

"Who are you?" Leine asked, keeping her gun hidden.

"The cleaning lady. I was told no one would be here today, so I came in." The woman glanced around nervously. "Is that all right?"

"Of course. I'm sorry I startled you. Please, go ahead," Leine replied.

The woman lowered her hand, her relief obvious. "I'll start in the offices down the hall so I won't bother you." Her smile was tentative as she glanced behind Leine into Greg's office. She cocked her head, a quizzical expression on her face. "Are you a new employee of Mr. Kirchner's?"

"Yes. Brand new. Now, if you'll excuse me, I need to get back to what I was doing."

She nodded, but Leine could tell she was curious about her. "Okay. I'll wait with the vacuuming until last."

"I'd appreciate it. Thank you."

The woman hurried down the hallway and Leine jogged back to the reception area. They had to leave, now, before the woman contacted someone to check on Leine's presence.

"Yuri. Time to go."

There was no answer. Leine moved past the front desk and down the hall to a room labeled *Employees Only*. She opened the door to a small office with a bank of three split-screen monitors along one wall, a desk and chair stationed in front of them. There was no sign of Yuri. There was also no sign of anyone in the vicinity of the cameras, although the screen marked *elevator* was dark. Leine reached over to disconnect the digital feed to the camera for the rear entrance and left.

After checking several of the offices with no luck, she returned to the reception area and cracked the front door open. The hall was empty. Leine pulled her gun free and closed the door behind her. She headed for the stairs, wondering where the hell Yuri had gone. The idiot could have compromised their position. She was careful to check the stairwell below her as she made her way to the first floor and hurried out the door to her car.

She peeled off her gloves and looked back at the building once more to see if he was somewhere nearby before driving away. He wasn't.

Yuri was on his own.

Yuri backed away from the man with the switchblade as the walls of the elevator closed in around him, his mind filled with dread at his mistake in avoiding the stairs. While he was watching the monitors in the control room two men had entered through the building's front door and took the stairs. Not recognizing either of them, panic got the better of him. Yuri escaped through the emergency exit at the rear of the office and raced for the elevator, not stopping long enough to warn Leine.

Bad decision.

The man in the elevator lunged forward and Yuri barely turned in time, the knife slicing through air. He reached for his gun, but was unable to pull it out before the man attacked a second time. A searing pain, unknown to him before now, radiated though Yuri's body as his attacker buried the blade in his stomach. Yuri doubled over in agony as the man recovered the knife and plunged it again and again into his shoulder, his back, his neck.

The doors to the elevator whispered open and his attacker stepped out, leaving Yuri gasping on the floor.

As his life ebbed from his body, Yuri lay in a pool of blood, staring at the wall above him. On it someone had taped a flier announcing a seminar on becoming rich through real estate.

The elevator door slid closed.

CHAPTER THIRTY-SIX

L EINE SLOWED AS SHE APPROACHED the address on Mulholland and picked up the little black box lying on the seat beside her. The iron security gate was equipped with a camera and key pad. When she was close enough, she aimed the jamming device at the camera and pulled up to the key pad as the light blinked off. She entered the password she'd gotten from Greg's computer and the gate swung open. The monitoring agency would likely log the incident regarding the malfunctioning camera, but probably wouldn't notify the owner since the correct entry code had been used.

She drove slowly up the long, winding driveway, past towering eucalyptus trees and manicured grounds, and parked just out of sight of the large timber frame and stone house at the top of the hill. Two cars were parked in the circular drive; a white commercial van with no signage and a black town car. Noting two security cameras at the front entrance, she silently crossed the yard to the side of the house and crouched beneath a window in the shadow of a boxwood shrub.

The furnishings consisted of white vintage 1950s chairs grouped around a low, intricately carved cocktail table, sitting on a thick, expensive looking rug. A large, silver mirror graced the far wall, with abstract paintings strategically placed among richly woven tapestries. An art glass chandelier hung from the ceiling.

Not seeing anyone, Leine moved toward the rear of the house. A massive patio with an outdoor kitchen surrounded an Olympic-sized pool with a pair of French doors leading inside the home. Tennis courts lay across the rolling lawn with graceful fichus trees punctuating the grounds. The afternoon light was fading, leaving long shadows in its wake. She moved into position under another window to get a better visual.

The rear section of the house was evidently used as a family room of sorts, with overstuffed leather chairs and a large sectional near the window. A pool table and wet bar stood at the far end next to several bookshelves.

Movement in her periphery caught Leine's eye and she slid into the shadows. Selena walked into the room and perched on the arm of one of the overstuffed chairs, ramrod straight, her expression tense. A solidly built man with spiky hair and a tailored, dark gray suit followed her into the room, crossed the floor to the wet bar and proceeded to make himself a drink. Another man with a dark complexion and a thick neck, wearing a black shirt and khakis came in next. The man with the spiky hair carried his drink over to where Selena was sitting. Leine started to slide her phone out of her pocket to call 911, but stopped when she noticed the dark-haired man walk up behind Selena, a garrote stretched between his hands.

Leine stepped from the shadows and aimed her gun through the window at the man with the garrote. The dull pop of the suppressed gunshot was followed by the tinkle of breaking glass. The man's head snapped backward, a dark hole no bigger than a dime on his forehead. The garrote fell from his grasp as he collapsed to the floor.

"Security!" the man with the spiked hair screamed and dove behind one of the chairs. Selena dropped to the floor on all fours and crawled under the coffee table. Leine ran around the corner of the house and burst through the French doors, ducking right as another man came rushing into the room with a gun. Leine shot him in the throat and took cover behind the pool table as he went down. The man in the suit scuttled across the floor like a crab, putting the chair between himself and Leine. Leine skirted the pool table to get a better vantage point for the next wave, keeping her eye on the man behind the chair, the doorway and windows.

Outside, two men with weapons ran past the window and took up position on each side of the French doors. Leine pivoted and fired through the glass, hitting one in the shoulder. The other ducked out of sight, then reappeared and fired several rounds. Leine dropped to a crouch as a bullet buried itself in the edge of the pool table next to her head. The guy in the suit made a dash for the doorway. Leine took aim from under the table and fired, splintering the jamb, but missed him. He disappeared into the hall.

Leine let him go and worked her way to the bookcase next to the doors, staying out of view of the second gunman. He inched upward to see where she was. She lunged forward and slammed her gun against the glass pane next to him, knocking shards into his face and temporarily blinding him before she fired, bringing him down. She checked outside for the man she'd shot through the shoulder, but he was nowhere to be seen.

Leine strode back inside the house and over to where Selena was hiding underneath the coffee table.

"You need to come out, Selena," Leine said.

She backed out and sat on her heels. Looking up at Leine, tears streamed down her face. Her hands shook as she clasped them together. "Please don't kill me. I...I had to do it. They have my little sister." She buried her face in her hands, sobbing. "I never would have done it. Never. They were going to—"

Leine reached down and grabbed Selena by the arm, jerking her to her feet. "Pull yourself together. Where's Mara?"

Fresh tears spilled over and down her cheeks. "In the basement. They locked her in a sound-proof room. There are more men."

"How many?"

"Three that I saw, plus Greg. I recognized one of them—he's Greg's personal security guard. I couldn't tell if the other two were armed."

"Which one's Greg?"

"The man who ran from the room just now."

"The guy with the hair?"

She nodded. "Yes. One of the other men is the buyer."

"How do you know that? Did he identify himself?"

Selena locked eyes with Leine. "He told everyone to leave, that he wanted to 'break her in'."

Leine shoved her toward the door and at the same time pulled out her phone. She scanned the grounds. The man she'd just killed lay on the patio near the French doors, but she didn't see anyone else. "You need to go before the others come."

216

Selena shook her head, her voice panicked. "No. I can't leave. I don't know where my sister is. I have to find her." More tears spilled over as she tried to pull away.

Leine backed up a few paces and glanced down the hallway. So far, no one else was coming. "Selena, listen to me." She snapped her fingers at the distraught woman, but she kept looking between the hall and the door, not focusing on Leine. Frustrated, Leine grabbed her by the chin, forcing her to look into her eyes. "You need to hide somewhere until the cops show up. When this is over, we can both make sure they know about her. Okay?" Selena nodded that she understood. Leine pushed her toward the door. "Now, go."

Selena took a step, but hesitated. Her voice wavered. "Her name is Amy. She's nine years—"

There was a popping sound from the patio. Shards of glass splintered onto the floor as a series of bullets burst through the window. Selena cried out and grabbed her side, a dark, red blood stain spreading beneath her fingers. The next rounds hit the wall next to Leine. A lamp and several picture frames attached to the wall shattered. She dove under the pool table and rolled, coming out the other side in a crouch. Her breath caught at the excruciating pain that radiated from her ribs. Blood pounding in her ears, she pushed past the throbbing ache and raised her gun, trying to locate the source of the shots.

Eyes wide with shock, Selena fell to her knees and onto her side, curling into a fetal position next to the French doors, blocking entry. She was still alive, evidenced by the rise and fall of her rib cage. A shadow crossed in front of one of the windows. Leine fired. Bullets ricocheted off the floor in front of her.

Leine quickly backed out of the room and called 911.

"State your emergency," the woman on the other end of the line requested.

"Shots fired, 88838 Mulholland Drive. Two gunmen down, presumed dead. One armed, but wounded. There's an unarmed Caucasian female severely wounded, approximately twenty-seven years old. We need an ambulance." Her side hurt like hell and she could barely take a breath, making it hard to talk. She worked to contain the adrenaline flowing through her body. "There are three others in the house who may be armed. I'm a Caucasian female, five-ten with auburn hair, wearing black slacks and a black jacket. My name is Leine Basso and I am armed. A twelve-year-old girl is in immediate danger and I'm going inside to find her. Tell your officers not to shoot me. Contact Detective Santiago Jensen. He knows the particulars."

"Officers are on their way."

Leine disconnected. Someone was coming down the hall.

CHAPTER THIRTY-SEVEN

LEINE SLIPPED INTO THE SHADOW of a doorway. Her opponent's movement was cautious, the owner intent on surprise. Quieting her breathing, she waited. The tremor she'd noticed before in her hand returned.

The steps slowed and then paused as though the assailant was uncertain whether to continue. Enveloped in shadow, Leine had the advantage, but the narrow hallway restricted her options. There'd be no room for error.

The footsteps resumed, the pace even more wary. Leine waited until she saw the barrel of the gun in the dim light. She exploded from the doorway, hitting him hard, and knocked the gun from his hand. The weapon skipped across the tile. At first surprised, his expression hardened. He came forward, swinging his right hand, his left hanging lifelessly by his side. She stepped right and his fist slammed into the wall behind her. Leine shifted again to the right, raised her gun and fired.

The gunman grunted as he spiraled backwards before falling to the floor, taking out a hall table on his way down. Too much noise, she thought, as she reached down to check his pulse. His left shoulder was covered in blood. He was the same man she'd shot through the shoulder on the patio. Assured he wouldn't give her any more trouble, she sprinted down the hallway toward the main part of the house. Outside, the sound of wheels on gravel told her someone was leaving. It had to be Greg. Of course he'd run. Why stay and fight? He'd successfully delivered Mara to his client. His job was done.

Leine ran through the cavernous kitchen, searching for the stairs. She found them on the other side of the dining room and quietly descended to the lower floor, caution overriding her desire to find Mara and get her out of the house before anything happened to her.

She wasn't sure if the man she'd just killed in the upstairs hallway was the same man who'd shot Selena through the window. Was he one of the men Selena said she saw in the basement? That would mean there were either two or three left. It wasn't Greg or the buyer, so that left Greg's security guy and possibly another man. Leine ejected the nearly empty magazine from her gun into her palm, pulled a full one from her jacket pocket and snapped it into place.

At the bottom of the steps was a large space with more overstuffed furniture and a built-in media center, the panels open to reveal a flat screen. To her left was a short hallway with two doors: one at the end led to a garage, the other opened onto a utility room. To the right was a longer corridor with several doors. She walked down the carpeted hallway, methodically checking inside each room.

She came to a set of double doors and listened to make sure no one was on the other side. When she didn't hear anything, she eased it open and looked in the spacious room.

Two movie cameras on dollies stood at either side of a king-sized bed, giving Leine a strong sense of *déjà vu*. Studio lighting, resembling that used on television shows, had been installed. Electrical cords snaked across the floor, secured to the carpeting with wide strips of gaffer's tape. The walls had been painted a delicate pink and fresh flowers stood in a vase on top of a bedside table.

This is where the bastard acts out his twisted fantasies. Fighting the bile that rose in her throat, Leine backed out of the room and closed the door.

The blow to her elbow took her by surprise. She barely managed to keep her hold on the gun as the numbness shot through her forearm and wrist. She whirled around, supporting the semiautomatic with both hands, but was met with another strike, this time from above. The gun fell soundlessly to the floor. She recognized her attacker.

Rico.

Leine stepped away as his foot snapped up, barely missing her face. She grabbed for his heel, but he dropped and rolled backward into a somersault, regaining his footing. Head down, he came at her and they both fell to the floor. Leine rolled clear of him and pushed to her feet, clamping her mouth closed to keep from crying out. Rico scrambled to his feet and lunged for her. His hand shot out, heel first, aiming at her throat. She dodged to the side as she knocked his hand away and latched onto his fingers, bending them back until he cried out.

"I should have known you'd be part of this, Rico. Scumbags always seem to stick together." Leine struggled to catch her breath. Each inhalation burned like fire. "What's your part in this? You like little girls, too?"

"Fuck you, Leine. You don't know shit," Rico said, and sagged to his knees, gasping.

"I know there's an innocent little girl somewhere in this house who isn't going to be the starring attraction in some pervert's warped idea of a blockbuster." Leine gave his hand a vicious twist before she shoved him onto his back with her foot. She retrieved her gun from the floor and walked back to where Rico was struggling to rise. He stopped moving when he saw the barrel of the gun pointed at him. "You gave the traffickers the information about Miles, didn't you?"

Rico looked away.

She stepped closer. "That's it, isn't it? How much did Greg pay you?"

He turned his head toward her, his expression defiant. "It was easy to convince Miles that Selena was his sister. He's an idiot. I taught her everything I knew about him and let me tell you, it was extensive. He's like a fucking open book. No one would've been the wiser if he'd listened to me and fired you when I told him to."

"This is a little girl's *life* we're talking about, here, Rico. Not a movie deal." Leine resisted the urge to smash her gun against his head. "Where's Mara?"

Rico sneered. "Like I'd tell you, bitch."

Leine bent over and shoved the gun against his forehead. "I don't have time for this, asshole. Where are they keeping the girl?"

Rico's eyes shifted right. "She's not here."

"You're lying." She pressed the barrel harder into his skull. "As you can see, the gun has a suppressor on it. No one will hear when I kill you."

Beads of sweat appeared on Rico's forehead, but he remained silent.

The faint sound of sirens wailed in the distance. Leine let up on the pressure and took a step back. "Okay, Rico. I'm sure the police will be able to squeeze the information out of you when they get here, but I doubt they'll go very easy on you. I'll be sure to tell them how well you cooperated. I imagine it will be hard to service clients from prison. "

Rico closed his eyes and swallowed. "Last door on the right," he finally replied.

"Thanks, Rico. You're quite the standup guy." She closed the distance between them. "This might hurt," she warned, and slammed the gun into his temple. Rico's eyes rolled back in his head and he collapsed to the floor. "At least, I hope so."

Leine raced to the end of the corridor and stopped at the last door on the right. She tried the handle, but it was locked. Both the door and the surrounding frame looked to be constructed of reinforced steel. She gently rapped her knuckles alongside the frame, then stepped back and fired several shots into the wall, blasting a hole through it next to the doorknob. Then she reached inside, unlocked the door and pushed it open.

A shirtless Stone Ellison stood on the far side of the room, next to a tall dresser, indignation and anger apparent on his face. His expression changed to disbelief when he saw Leine's gun. A flat screen T.V. hung against one wall, the images flashing across it the subject of which Leine would never forget. Mara sat huddled and shaking against the headboard of the king-sized bed, tears streaming down her face, gripping the bedcovers to her chin. A frilly white sundress adorned with tiny pink bows lay next to her.

The muffled sound of people yelling on the floor above them told her the police had arrived. Keeping the gun trained on Ellison, Leine held out her hand. "You're safe now, Mara."

With a sob, Mara slid off the bed and ran to her, throwing her arms around her and burying her face in her side. Leine was relieved to see she still wore a tee shirt and underwear. She pulled off her jacket and wrapped it around the young girl's shoulders, watching the man standing in the corner with contempt. Ellison's arrogant expression faltered as the full import of what was happening hit him.

"I'd shoot you now if I wasn't certain your time in prison would be the worst kind of hell. Pedophiles don't usually do very well." With one last glance at the monster in the corner, Leine turned and gently took Mara by the hand, leading her out into the hallway, away from Ellison.

The first of several uniformed officers reached the bottom of the stairs and started toward them, guns drawn.

"Drop your gun and step away from the girl," the one in front shouted as he moved past Rico's inert body.

Leine tossed her gun to the floor and raised her hands above her head. "I'm the one that called. My name is Leine Basso." She glanced at Mara as she backed away from the frightened little girl. The terror on her face almost broke Leine's heart. "It's all right, Mara. Don't be afraid. This will all be over soon."

Mara stood alone in the middle of the hallway, her whole body shaking. She turned to look at Leine. "Please don't let them take me back," she said, tears coursing down her face.

"I won't, honey. I promise."

224

CHAPTER THIRTY-EIGHT

LEINE WALKED UP TO THE familiar wooden doors and rang the doorbell. No M-4 carrying security detail greeted her this time. A few moments later the door opened and a grinning Miles appeared. He stepped forward and wrapped her in a gentle hug, then released her.

"Glad you could make it. We're in the back, by the pool. April and Cory are already here."

Miles led her down the hallway, through the kitchen and out the door to the patio. Clusters of people stood chatting with each other, many of whom Leine had met during her time as Miles' bodyguard. Out on the lawn, several older children kicked a soccer ball back and forth. The pool was alive with splashing, screaming kids of all ages, throwing bright-colored beach balls at each other, their parents relaxing on the chaise lounges, enjoying the warm day. April saw Leine and waved. She and Cory sat together at a table with another couple next to the pool.

A waiter walked by with a tray of festive drinks. Miles grabbed two and offered Leine one.

She took a sip and looked at him in surprise. "No tequila?"

He shrugged. "Thought I should tone things down, now that I'm going to be a dad."

At that moment, Mara came running up to them and threw her arms around Leine in a giant bear hug. "I'm so glad you're here! Look what Miles got me." She held out a shiny new iPad. "It holds tons of books and music and stuff."

"Yeah, she's working on her library," Miles said, pride mixed with tenderness evident in his voice.

"That's pretty cool, Mara," Leine said.

Mara beamed. A boy who looked to be about her age came up and whispered something in her ear. She giggled and nodded. "Aiden wants me to come and play soccer," she said, by way of explanation.

"You should ask April and Cory if they'd like to play. They both love soccer," Leine suggested.

"All right. I will." Mara bounded down the stairs toward the pool, Aiden in tow.

"She looks happy," Leine said, watching them. She turned to Miles. "And so do you. How are things going with the adoption?"

"Should be happening soon. Her biological mother can't be located. It seems she didn't leave a forwarding address after Mara was put into foster care, and there's no information on the father's whereabouts." A look of sadness skated across his face, but it was soon replaced with a smile. "The next hurdle is a site visit, but they've told me it's just a technicality. It should only be a matter of weeks until Mara gets to come home permanently."

"That's great, Miles. I'm glad."

"How's Selena? Is she out of the hospital yet?"

"The doctors are shooting for next Friday. She's lucky to be alive."

"I doubt she'll think so when she finds out Greg hasn't told the police where to find her sister."

"Yeah." Leine gazed out at the rolling hills and sighed. Not finding Amy was an unacceptable loose end. Leine really hated loose ends, especially when it involved a child. She'd already put a couple of calls in to see if she could find out anything. One of her contacts had uncovered a couple of promising leads. "I heard the D.A. told him they'd float him a deal if he gives up the names of his clients. They might be able to find her that way."

"So there's hope." Miles gave her a half-hearted smile and took a sip of his drink.

"I was wondering when you were going to get here."

Leine turned at the sound of the familiar voice. Santiago Jensen walked over and put his arm around her waist. He leaned in to give her a chaste kiss on the cheek and whispered, "How long did you want to stay?"

"Haven't we left yet?" Leine laughed and slipped her hand in his as she turned toward their host. "Thank you for inviting us, Miles, but something's come up and we're going to have to leave."

Miles narrowed his eyes at them and grinned. "Thanks for coming, at least for a few minutes. I'll call you next week. We'll do lunch." He put his hand to his ear like a telephone. "Have fun, you two," he added, and walked over to join a group of people chatting nearby.

Leine and Jensen walked hand in hand through the crowd, back into the house.

"To what do I owe this surprise?" Leine asked as he opened the front door for her and they walked outside.

"They dropped the murder charges. The files checked out."

Finally. It was a bittersweet victory. Carlos was still dead. "And what about Eric?"

Jensen shrugged. "What about him? The poor bastard was in the wrong place at the wrong time. Gang activity in that area has been escalating. He shouldn't have been there alone in the first place."

Leine felt her shoulders relax. She was in the clear, free to be with Jensen without having to look over her shoulder. "What's going to happen to Ellison?"

"He'll do some serious time. Turns out he's part of a group involved in international child pornography. They trade videos between themselves and identify members by wearing a distinctive ring. The task force is working with Interpol and designated a special team to go after the others."

Leine leaned her head back to feel the sun on her face and took a deep breath of fresh air. Mara was safe and would soon be adopted, giving her a home and Miles the family he'd always longed for. Greg and his 'talent agency' were history. His computer and files had been confiscated, and investigators were combing through them to find out how far his network reached, as well as piecing together who the victims were.

There were still so many out there who needed help, but it was a start. Her friend Lou had asked her if she'd be interested in working with SHEN, helping to locate missing children. Leine had already decided she would. With her background and skill set it was a natural fit.

Sometimes, she thought, things really do work out.

THE END

HUMAN TRAFFICKING STATISTICS:

o According to the U.S. State Department, more than *two million people* are trafficked worldwide every year. Eighty percent of these victims are exploited for sexual slavery; fifty percent are minors.

o Human trafficking is the fastest growing criminal enterprise in the world with profits in excess of $32 billion, second only to the illegal drug trade. (*U.S. State Department*)

o As many as 2.8 million children run away each year in the US. Within 48 hours, one-third of these children are lured or recruited into the underground world of prostitution and pornography. (*National Center for Missing and Exploited Children*)

o Experts estimate that 100,000-300,000 American children are at risk of becoming victims of commercial child prostitution; girls as young as 12 and boys as young as 11 are being victimized. (*NCMEC*).

o Child pornography is one of the fastest growing crimes in the United States. Nationally, there has been a 2500% increase in arrests in 10 years. (*FBI*).

To learn more, visit these websites:

- Polaris Project: www.polarisproject.org
- Truckers Against Trafficking: www.truckersagainsttrafficking.com
- Federal Bureau of Investigation: www.fbi.gov
- United Nations Office on Drugs and Crime (UNODC): www.unodc.org
- National Center for Missing & Exploited Children: www.mcnec.org

ABOUT THE AUTHOR:
DV Berkom is a slave to the voices in her head. As the bestselling author of two award-winning thriller series (*Leine Basso* and *Kate Jones*), her love of creating resilient, kick-ass women characters stems from a lifelong addiction to reading spy novels, mysteries, and thrillers, and longing to find the female equivalent within those pages.

Raised in the Midwest, she received a BA in political science from the University of Minnesota and promptly moved to Mexico to live on a sailboat. Many, many cross-country moves later, she now lives just outside of Seattle, Washington with the love of her life, Mark, a-chef-turned-contractor, and several imaginary characters who love to tell her what to do.

To find out more, please visit her website at www.dvberkom.com.

More works by DV Berkom:
Leine Basso Thriller Series:
Serial Date (Leine Basso #1)
The Body Market (Leine Basso #3)
Cargo (Leine Basso #4)
Kate Jones Thriller Series:
Bad Spirits (novella #1)
Dead of Winter (novella #2)
Death Rites (novella #3)
Touring for Death (novella #4)
Cruising for Death (book #5)
Yucatán Dead (book #6)
A One Way Ticket to Dead (book #7)

DV BERKOM

A LEINE BASSO THRILLER

THE BODY
MARKET

EXCERPT FROM THE NEXT LEINE BASSO THRILLER
THE BODY MARKET

CHAPTER 1

LEINE BASSO CROUCHED in the shadows next to the hulking metal shipping container. The odor of oil mixed with hydraulic fluid and diesel clashed with the briny sea air. Bright spotlights pierced the darkness casting a harsh yellow hue over the container yard. Leine checked her watch: eleven o'clock. Only three hours before the *China Blue Star* was scheduled to leave port for Hong Kong.

Three hours to find one shipping container in a massive sea of identical containers.

Lou paid off the security guard, which gave Leine only a short window to find the container before he released the dogs. She adjusted the fit of the pack, tightening the straps so it molded to her body. She'd pared down the equipment as much as she could, but it was never enough.

C'mon, Lou. Give me some good news.

She closed her eyes and imagined the young face in the photograph. A lead from the trafficker's hard drive had led her to a seaport currently run by cartel thugs on the west coast of Mexico. She hoped she wasn't too late.

Three hours.

"Leine." Lou's voice came over the wireless earpiece.

"I'm here," she replied.

"Left, three aisles, number fourteen-thirty-four-twelve."

"Got it." Gun drawn and keeping to the shadows, Leine moved along first one aisle, then another, searching for shipping container 143412.

There it is.

Stacked three high, the 40 foot-long steel boxes loomed above her. The one she was looking for was stacked 40 feet in the air on top of two other boxes. She moved to the end of the bottom container and reached for a handhold. Before she could grab the next one, someone seized her pack and yanked her off, slamming her back-first into the pavement. Her nine millimeter skittered across the asphalt, disappearing in the darkness between two containers. The impact took her breath away, the pain from a recent rib injury spiking through her like a spear.

Leine rolled, narrowly missing a kick to the face. She grabbed her attacker's foot and gave it a vicious twist. The assailant corkscrewed and landed on his side with a grunt.

Ignoring the deep ache in her side and with adrenaline fueling her, she sprang to her feet and kicked the gun from his hand. The weapon pinged off the side of the container and bounced into the shadows, out of sight. Before she could get clear, he scissored his legs and caught her at the knees. She sprawled forward.

This time she couldn't ignore the pain.

Winded, she slid a knife free from the sheath attached to her leg. She pushed off the ground, rolling to a crouch as her opponent climbed to his feet, a knife in his hand. He lunged forward. Leine parried with a thrust to his throat. At the last second, he ducked.

They circled each other like roosters in a cockfight, both acutely aware of the weapon in their opponent's grip. Leine feinted left and rushed forward, scoring a direct hit on the man's shoulder, slicing through the black fabric of his shirt and drawing blood. He pivoted and came at her from the side but she rotated her torso, narrowly missing a slash to her kidney. She turned to face him as he came at her again. At the last second she stepped wide, allowing him to slip past her. Using his own momentum, she shoved him forward. He stumbled a few steps, recovered, and spun to face her.

Leine swept her arm forward in an arc and released the knife. The blade buried itself in his eye socket, a scream dying in his throat as his hand flew reflexively to his face. He collapsed to the ground as he exhaled his last breath.

"Leine. What's going on? Are you okay?" Usually unflappable, the sharpness in Lou's voice betrayed his concern, even over the radio.

"I'm fine." Her hand supporting her now-throbbing rib, she leaned over the body with a grimace and extracted the knife, wiping the blade on the dead man's shirt. The tattoos on his forearm suggested cartel affiliation. Leine doubted he was working alone. "Just some unexpected company."

"Did you find the container?"

Leine scanned the metal boxes above her.

"Got it."

"I don't have to tell you to be careful, right?"

"No, but it's nice to know you care."

Leine grabbed the man's legs and gritted her teeth as she dragged the body into the dark gap between containers. She removed his transmitter, turned off the voice activation, and slid on the earpiece. She didn't want the next gunman to come along and sound the alarm before she had a chance to subdue him. After she retrieved the weapons she checked to see that the body couldn't be observed from the aisle. Satisfied, she walked back to container 143412.

With a quick glance to be sure the fight hadn't attracted company, she latched onto a vertical handle at the end of the first container, wedged her toe onto a hinge, and began to climb.

As she was preparing to hoist herself up and over the top of the container, she heard movement below her and froze.

"Where are you?" the voice muttered in Spanish, clear enough for Leine to hear through the transmitter.

She craned her neck, trying to catch a glimpse of the man below her. Compact in bearing and dressed in black like the man she'd just killed, instead of a knife he carried a modified submachine gun.

"Answer me," he snapped into his earpiece. When he received no reply, the man stepped over the smear of blood left by his compatriot. It looked like he might continue on when he abruptly stopped. Leine held her breath. If he glanced down, he'd notice the blood. With her left foot wedged onto the barest of toeholds and gripping the top of the container with her left hand, Leine slid her gun out of its holster, ready to fire—something she was loath to do since the sound would bring others.

The man pivoted 180 degrees, scanning the area, his gun in front of him. Leine ignored the muscles screaming in her left hand as the metal cut into her flesh.

He stood still for another moment, observing his surroundings. After a few seconds, he touched his earpiece.

"He's not here." The person at the other end acknowledged the transmission. "I'll keep looking," the gunman said as he moved out of Leine's line of sight.

She released her breath in a quiet sigh and slid the gun back into her shoulder holster. With her right hand now free, she grabbed onto the top of the container, relieving her left hand. She waited a couple of beats to make sure the gunman was clear and then pulled herself up and over.

The higher vantage point worked well to monitor the yard. When the other gunman had traveled far enough that he wouldn't hear her, Leine shrugged out of her pack and set it aside. She stretched flat onto her belly and put her ear to the container. There was no discernible movement inside.

That didn't mean much.

"I'm on the roof," she said in a low voice.

"Hear anything?" Lou asked.

"No."

Leine unzipped the main compartment of the bag and pulled out a battery pack and a mini plasma cutter and placed them on the roof beside her. Next, she reached into another compartment for a fiber optic night vision camera and a collapsible light hood.

She deployed the hood and marked the area to be cut, then flipped the plasma cutter's switch to on and adjusted the amps. Angling the tip as she cut, the small hole took only a few minutes. Turning off the cutter, she stowed it back inside the pack along with the hood.

Alert for movement on the ground below her, she activated the camera and fed the probe through the hole, watching the video feed on the small LCD monitor as she did. At first, all she could make out were the metal ribs of the container. She fed the line further into the dark interior and a moment later the camera swept past an object. Leine pulled up on the scope to get a better look. The object moved. Two tiny light circles appeared and blinked off and on.

As she angled the camera for a better view, she realized she was looking at a dark-haired girl huddled in the corner, her eyes glowing dots in the camera's lens. Leine pulled back for a wider shot. Dozens of bodies came into focus, placed side by side on the floor of the container with no room between them. Most were lying prone—except for the young girl.

"I've got something," Leine said into the mic.

Lou let out a sigh as though he'd been holding his breath.

Another girl, this one with light-colored hair, sat up and looked first at the girl in the corner and then at the camera.

Leine's heart beat faster. From what she could tell, she matched the picture.

Amy.

"Is she there?" Lou's clipped tone gave away his anxiety.

"Yeah. I think so. And she's not alone."

Leine relaxed her shoulders, relief flooding through her.

"Let's get them out of here, Lou."

CHAPTER 2

ELISE WAVED A fistful of pesos at the bartender in an attempt to flag him down. She stood her ground as the press of spring-breakers surged against her, pushing her into the crowded, mile-long chrome bar. The oppressive heat from the packed club combined with the pulsating music from the nearby speakers reminded Elise of an old movie from the seventies she'd seen a few nights before, and not in a good way. The bartender raced past, his dark eyes barely registering her.

Earlier, when Josh had been with her, the bartender had gushed over them both. That was over two hours ago. The bar wasn't as busy then. With an impatient sigh, she lowered her arm. Elise was not used to being ignored when money was involved. In her world, currency was king. Both her parents ran with an elite crowd even for Angelenos—the A-Listers of the financial world. Her father was the head of a thriving biotech company about to go public, and her mother worked as a financial consultant, dealing primarily in hedge fund management. Both ultra-busy professionals, neither had time to spend with their seventeen-year-old daughter. Elise preferred it that way. If she needed an adult, which was rare, she went to the housekeeper, Teuta, a grandmotherly woman from some Eastern European country Elise had never heard of.

"I'll only be gone five minutes," Josh, her date for the evening had said, and disappeared with some guy he'd just met at the bar. That had been two hours ago. Elise was now officially bored.

And pissed.

Giving up on getting a drink within the next millennium, she shoved the money back in her Louis Vuitton clutch and squeezed past the crush of wasted partiers. Teuta would be horrified to know her little Eliseka had crossed the border from Southern California into Mexico with a boy she hardly knew, ending the evening alone at a bar in Tijuana.

Unable to locate Josh anywhere in the club, Elise made her way to the exit, pushing disgustedly at the ogling drunks who staggered up to her. Apparently they'd never seen a blonde wearing a low-cut, sparkly dress and five-inch Louboutin heels.

So juvenile, she thought.

Outside, the heat from the unseasonably hot spring day radiated off the sidewalk into the evening air and mixed with the nauseating smell of car fumes and cigarettes. Brash neon from the row of nightclubs lit the street as though it were daylight, casting everyone around her in a sickly kaleidoscopic glow. People milled past, laughing as they hurried to the next bar. Her anger growing, Elise dug her phone out of her purse and called her best friend, Brittany.

"Hey—what's up?"

Elise plugged an ear, unable to hear over the music blasting from the club behind her.

"Josh left me at the bar."

"Seriously? He is so dead."

"Yeah. Listen. Can you come and pick me up?"

"Of course, sweetie. I can be at the border in a couple of hours."

"Sorry. Didn't mean to ruin your Saturday night."

"Believe me, you didn't ruin it. I'm happy to get out of town. There's *nothing* going on."

Elise ended the call, slipped the phone back into her purse, and turned to wave down a taxi. It wasn't far to where she was going to meet her friend, but Elise didn't feel like walking and possibly breaking a heel. A cab immediately pulled to the curb and Elise walked over to the driver.

"How much to the border?" she asked.

The cab driver scanned her from head to toe and back again, his leer punctuated by a missing front tooth.

"For you, señorita, almost free."

Elise rolled her eyes. She turned and walked away, ignoring the slow crawl of the taxi behind her. She'd find another, more respectful driver.

"Come on, *chica*. I didn't mean anything by it."

Elise kept walking. The cab driver attempted to get her attention, but when he saw it wasn't working, sped past her.

"Elise! Wait."

Josh hurried toward her through the crowd, an apologetic smile on his face. She crossed her arms and glared at him.

"Babe, I'm so sorry. Please don't be mad. The guy had this killer weed, and I lost track of time and…"

"Are you kidding me? You left me alone in that club for two hours, Josh. *Two hours*. What the hell?"

Josh stepped closer to Elise, sliding his hand along her bare arm. The casual, thrown together look of his über-expensive T-shirt and jeans, along with the perfectly tousled, sun-kissed hair reminded her of a model she'd seen in a magazine advertising men's cologne.

"Aw, come on, babe. Don't be like that. I'll make it up to you." His grin brought out the dimples in his cheeks and Elise tried hard to suppress a smile. He was still the hottest guy she knew. So what if he was a little forgetful? It was probably the weed.

"See? I made you smile. I know you love me." Josh grinned, hugging Elise with one arm as he turned them around and headed in the opposite direction.

"Wait." Elise stopped. "Brittany's supposed to pick me up."

"So text her and tell her not to come. The guy told me about a sick party near Rosarito. Some movie star rented a house outside of town and is having an all-weekend bash. There's a band."

"Like who?" Elise wasn't impressed by most celebrities. Her mother did a lot of business with A-Listers in the film world, too. She couldn't think of many she'd go out of her way to meet.

"He didn't say who the actor was, but he told me Swarm of Nihilists is going to be there all weekend!" Josh did the Nihilist Salute fist pump. Elise almost rolled her eyes again. Josh was heavy into S.O.N.

"Fine. But can we leave if it's bullshit? I mean, how do you know this guy?"

Josh's earnest expression almost made her laugh. "He's a roadie for the Nihilists. He totally knows his shit."

Elise shook her head but after a few minutes of cajoling finally relented to Josh's pleas. They walked to where he had parked the Porsche his dad had given him as an early graduation present and were soon headed out of the city center toward the beach town of Rosarito. Elise texted Brittany, telling her to cancel her plans to come and get her.

r u sure? i can b there in 2 hrs, Brittany answered. *Josh is hot, but how well do u really know him?*

i'm sure. ty 4 worrying, she replied. Elise slipped the phone back in her purse. She knew all she needed to about Josh. He came from a wealthy family, was gorgeous, and drove an awesome car. Plus, he hadn't really abandoned her at the club. So what if she had to go to some party where she didn't know anybody? If Swarm of Nihilists actually turned out to be there she'd have a great story to tell her friends Monday morning during first period.

Josh wove through the back streets as though he knew where he was going. Elise relaxed and watched as they passed darkened dentists' offices and brightly lit neighborhood groceries. Locals had gathered near a popular *taqueria* with *banda* music blaring from a loudspeaker. Drunk high school and college kids crawled the alleys for forbidden excitement, all against a backdrop of colorful billboards that screamed cheap pharmaceuticals and even cheaper attorneys. The neighborhood thinned as they drove past the turnoff to the main freeway.

"Where are you going? Isn't that the way to the toll road?" Elise asked, looking behind them.

He reached inside his pocket and pulled out a book of matches. "The guy wrote down how to get there on the back of this." He handed her the directions. Elise turned on the overhead light to read them.

"He called it the library or something."

"You mean *libre*? The free road?" Elise shook her head. "You're not seriously trying to get out of paying the toll. What is it, like two bucks?"

"No, of course not." Josh frowned in irritation. "It's just that he said it'd be easier to find the house if we went this way."

"Who was this guy again?"

Earlier in the evening, the man with the Russian accent had started a conversation with Josh while they were at the bar waiting for drinks and had offered to get both Elise and him high. Elise had declined.

"A friend."

"A friend. And you've known him how long?"

Josh gave her a look. "You sound like my mom. Don't worry. It'll be fine. We're gonna see Swarm of Nihilists!"

With a resigned sigh, Elise leaned her head back and closed her eyes. The warm night air drifting through the window felt so much better than being inside the hot, stuffy bar. Thoughts of what she was going to wear to her friend Nicole's big party the next weekend filled her mind. She wasn't sure she wanted to invite Josh. She'd have to see who else was available. They'd look good together though, she'd give him that.

A few miles later, Josh had Elise read the directions out loud. He found the street and turned right, heading west along a gravel road. The car began to climb and they left the lights of the city below them.

"You're sure you know where you're going, right?" Elise asked, wondering why there weren't any streetlights.

"Yeah. He said it would look like we were heading nowhere but to just keep going to the top of the hill."

The road grew steeper and Josh shifted into second gear to get traction. Just as Elise was going to ask him to take her back, a dramatic white arch with black lettering loomed in the darkness before them.

"What does it say?" Josh asked.

Elise glanced at the lettering on the stucco façade as they passed underneath.

"Vista del Mar."

"That's it. He said it would be a little ways past that, and we'd see the house in front of us."

They continued along the gravel road. Hulking concrete skeletons of unfinished homes stood as brooding sentries on each side.

"Must be a really new development," Josh said, by way of explanation. Elise wasn't so sure. There were no building materials lying next to the houses, and she didn't see any heavy equipment.

"Where are the streetlights? You'd think there'd be something, right?"

Josh shrugged. "Who knows? Maybe that's the reason they decided to have the party here—less people, less hassle. Look—" Josh pointed through the windshield. "You can see the lights of Rosarito."

Elise's gaze followed his outstretched arm as he pointed at the bright lights of the seaside town far below them. She rummaged inside her purse for her phone as they drove further along the darkened street. She brought up the GPS and squinted at the lit LED screen, trying to figure out where they had ended up.

They turned a corner and Josh stopped the car. "What the fuck."

Elise looked up. The Porsche's headlights spilled across the road and onto an oversized, black SUV parked in front of them, blocking the way. Two flares burned bright orange in the expanse between the two vehicles. A muscular man with blond hair leaned against the truck, arms crossed, smoking a cigarette.

Confused, she turned to Josh. "What's going on?"

"I don't know."

"That isn't the guy from the bar, is it?"

Josh shook his head. "Uh-uh." He made to get out of the car, but she grabbed his arm.

"Don't. What if he wants to rob us?" Elise had heard stories about carjackings and highway robbery near the border. From what her friends had told her, those kinds of things weren't supposed to happen between Tijuana and Rosarito.

"He won't get much. I blew most of my money at the bar."

"Yeah, but you're driving an expensive car. He could steal it, and then we'd have to wait out here until someone comes to get us or walk all the way back." Elise glanced out her window at the deserted buildings nearby and shivered.

"Shit. I never thought of that." With a quick look behind them, Josh seized the gearshift and slammed the car into reverse. Elise braced her feet against the floor and gripped the armrest as Josh backed away, the tires spitting rocks.

Elise twisted in her seat to watch through the rear window. A second SUV came out of nowhere, bounced onto the road behind them, and blocked their escape. Elise screamed. Josh braked hard and the Porsche skidded to a stop.

"What should we do?" Elise's panicked voice sounded overly loud in the small space. She raised her window and locked her door. Josh did the same.

"*Shit.* I can't give them the car. My dad just gave it to me. He's gonna be so pissed." The whites of his eyes glistened in the glow from the dash. "What should I do?"

He's scared to death, she thought. Cold dread crept its way up her spine as she recalled the horror stories she'd read online. What if they figured out they both were from wealthy families? It wouldn't be hard, not with the kind of car they were in, or with what they were wearing. She glanced at Josh's expensive wristwatch, worth enough to feed a developing nation, and then at her shoes. The diamond chips on the heels twinkled in the darkness. What if they kidnapped them both and held them for ransom?

Jesus, Elise thought, her heart racing. *My parents don't even answer their phones unless it's business. They won't know what happened to me until it's too late.*

"Did you take a wrong turn?"

Josh shook his head. "I'm sure it was the right one. Maybe they just want us to turn around."

"I don't think so, Josh." A chilling thought flitted through Elise's mind. "The guy at the bar. He did this, didn't he? He saw your watch, or maybe he even knew what you were driving and decided to make some easy money."

Josh shook his head. "No. It's not like that, Lise. He was totally cool." His voice didn't sound as confident as it had just a short time ago. A sheen of sweat formed on his forehead.

The man with the cigarette leaned down and picked something up off the ground. He flicked the butt away before he ambled over to the driver's side and tapped on the window. Josh stared straight ahead, his fingers clamped to the steering wheel.

"Get out," the man said, motioning at the door.

"Th-this isn't my car."

Josh's pleading tone grated on Elise's nerves. So not the guy she thought he was.

The man smiled benignly and stepped back. He raised his arms and something hard came crashing down across the windshield, buckling the glass. Josh jumped at the same time Elise screamed.

The man slammed the tire iron against the window again and again, methodically smashing through the safety glass. Then he moved near the front of the car and smashed the left headlight.

"Stop—!" Josh shouted, his voice a double octave higher than normal. "Not the *car.*"

The man stopped and walked back to Josh's window. He leaned against the fender and stared at him through the glass.

"Open the door." His muffled voice and bemused smile didn't lessen the impact of his demand. Josh was shaking, and his hands looked like they were going to choke the life out of the steering wheel. When he didn't respond, the man went to work on the side mirror.

At that moment, a second man appeared at Elise's window and she screamed. She closed her eyes and turned away, hunching her shoulders, afraid to look directly at the man standing next to her and wincing at each blow of the tire iron.

The man outside her window tapped again, more insistently this time. Her breath now coming in short bursts, Elise opened her eyes to slits and slowly turned her head, hoping that the scene before her could be controlled by what she did or didn't allow herself to see.

Her stomach lurched at the sight of a gun against the window. She closed her eyes again and shook her head.

Tap, tap, tap. Hot tears spilled down her cheeks as Elise gripped her knees to control her shaking hands.

"Get out of the car. Now." The man's menacing tone made it clear it wasn't a request.

"We'd better do as they say, Lise." Near tears and trembling, Josh reached for the door.

"No, Josh. *Don't.*"

But it was too late. He opened the door and climbed out. The first man seized him by the arm and shoved him away from the car and onto his knees, aiming a gun at his head. With the weapon still trained on Josh, he reached inside the car and unlocked Elise's door.

"No!" Elise screamed as the second man wrenched the door open, grabbed her by the hair, and yanked her out of the car. She landed hard on the gravel beside the

Porsche. A sharp pain lanced down her leg, followed by the warm, sticky-wetness of blood.

Elise didn't have time to gain her feet before the man grabbed her around the waist and lifted her off the ground. She kicked and squirmed and tried to rake his face with her nails as he dragged her away from the car, losing one of her shoes in the process, but the man never faltered. The moment before he shoved her into the back of the open SUV, Elise managed to twist around and look back at Josh.

Shoulders shaking and head bowed, his wristwatch glinted in the moonlight. A light breeze ruffled his hair.

"Take my car. I promise I won't report it if you let me go," he pleaded with the man in front of him.

"I thought you said it wasn't your car," the man replied with a smile as he moved behind him.

"I lied. I'm scared. Please don't kill me. I—I'm only eighteen." Sobbing now, Josh put his hands up as though they were playing a game and it was time to quit. Elise held her breath. Overwhelming fear tightened her chest and spread to her throat, the nausea in her stomach gaining momentum.

Before she could utter a sound, the man aimed the gun at the back of Josh's head.

And fired.

END EXCERPT